The cor
was flur

Bolan thrust himself to the side, rolled when he hit the ground and came up on one knee, his ice-blue eyes sweeping the terrain for more threats. A short volley from his M4 took down two more gunmen.

As he stood, Bolan loaded an HE round into the grenade launcher. He set his sights on a single-story building. An undulating glow of flames was visible inside the structure through the windows. A pair of bay doors that made up half of the building's facade were buckling from the onslaught of the flames.

The handful of guards, who had been trying to hose down the structure, abandoned their work when they saw Bolan and began grabbing for their weapons.

He noticed another man climbing frantically into the cab of a tanker truck and, judging by his urgency, Bolan guessed the truck wasn't filled with corn syrup.

The Executioner leveled the launcher and fired.

MACK BOLAN ®

The Executioner

The Executioner®
Don Pendleton's

BLOOD VENDETTA

A GOLD EAGLE BOOK FROM
W★RLDWIDE®

TORONTO • NEW YORK • LONDON
AMSTERDAM • PARIS • SYDNEY • HAMBURG
STOCKHOLM • ATHENS • TOKYO • MILAN
MADRID • WARSAW • BUDAPEST • AUCKLAND

Recycling programs
for this product may
not exist in your area.

First edition December 2012

ISBN-13: 978-0-373-64409-4

Special thanks and acknowledgment to
Tim Tresslar for his contribution to this work.

BLOOD VENDETTA

Printed in U.S.A.

Injustice anywhere is a threat to justice everywhere.
                                    —Martin Luther King, Jr.
                                              1929—1968

Sometimes to get justice, you need to go around the law.
Is this right or wrong? That's not for me to say. I am
no judge—I am the Executioner.
                                    —Mack Bolan

THE
MACK BOLAN
LEGEND

Nothing less than a war could have fashioned the destiny of the man called Mack Bolan. Bolan earned the Executioner title in the jungle hell of Vietnam.

But this soldier also wore another name—Sergeant Mercy. He was so tagged because of the compassion he showed to wounded comrades-in-arms and Vietnamese civilians.

Mack Bolan's second tour of duty ended prematurely when he was given emergency leave to return home and bury his family, victims of the Mob. Then he declared a one-man war against the Mafia.

He confronted the Families head-on from coast to coast, and soon a hope of victory began to appear. But Bolan had broken society's every rule. That same society started gunning for this elusive warrior—to no avail.

So Bolan was offered amnesty to work within the system against terrorism. This time, as an employee of Uncle Sam, Bolan became Colonel John Phoenix. With a command center at Stony Man Farm in Virginia, he and his new allies—Able Team and Phoenix Force—waged relentless war on a new adversary: the KGB.

But when his one true love, April Rose, died at the hands of the Soviet terror machine, Bolan severed all ties with Establishment authority.

Now, after a lengthy lone-wolf struggle and much soul-searching, the Executioner has agreed to enter an "arm's-length" alliance with his government once more, reserving the right to pursue personal missions in his Everlasting War.

Prologue

The soft, steady beeping roused her from a light sleep.

For a half second, she thought it was her alarm clock, waking her for work. The bank! Jesus, she needed to get up!

Her eyes snapped open. Reality sank in and, like an unseen hand, it jerked her upright in her bed. The lamp on her bedside table flickered on and off in time with the beeping.

By the time she threw aside her blankets, her heart was pounding in her chest, her mouth dry with fear.

Muttering a curse, she swung her legs over the side of the bed, hauled herself upright and padded across the floor to a laptop computer that stood on top of the white pine dresser. The computer, which was hooked into her alarm system, was in sleep mode. She punched a couple of buttons on the keyboard and the screen brightened. A window with a layout of each floor of the two-story home was displayed on the screen. A flashing red dot indicated a tripped sensor at the rear door.

Turning, she grabbed a pair of black denim jeans that were hung over the back of a chair and slipped them on, followed by a black turtleneck and sneakers.

It might be no big deal, she told herself as she laced up her shoes. The house was supposed to be empty. Maybe it was some teens looking for a place to drink or screw. Or a homeless man looking for a warm place to spend the night.

Or maybe someone had come for her. The thought caused blood to pound in her ears. Fear stuck in her throat as a dull but insistent ache.

No, she told herself, not this night. She set her jaw and shook her head to flush out the panicked thoughts. Returning to her bed, she kneeled next to it and felt around beneath it for the Smith & Wesson .38 revolver sheathed in a leather holster. Her memory raced back to the pawn shop where she'd purchased the weapon, to her conversation with the owner. He'd patiently explained that the .38 wasn't the most powerful handgun in the world, but it was simple and reliable. She'd tapped her finger against a glass case that contained four 9 mm auto-loading pistols.

"Aren't those better?" she'd asked. "More bullets?"

She'd at least known that much about guns at the time. The pawn shop owner, holding the S&W revolver, the empty cylinder flopped out to the side, flashed a nasty grin. He flicked his wrist and the cylinder snapped into place.

"Lady," he had said, "you can't put something down with five shots from this, save the sixth for yourself."

He'd laughed.

She'd swallowed hard and with barely another word bought the revolver, three speed loaders and two boxes of hollowpoint ammunition.

Years later, she still hadn't decided how much of what he'd said had been a joke aimed at further unnerving an already nervous lady and how much had been his true belief.

A night-light plugged into a wall outlet suddenly blinked.

The first alarm, which already had stopped beeping, was designed to wake her, alert her to an initial intrusion.

This one told her someone had set off motion detectors on the first floor. Belting the pistol around her waist, she reached under the bed again, feeling around until fingertips brushed against cold steel. She closed her hand around the shotgun barrel and pulled the weapon from beneath the bed.

The 20-gauge shotgun's double barrel had been sawed down to eighteen inches. Like the revolver, she liked the shotgun's simplicity. Easy to carry and load and unload. It didn't require marksmanship to hit a target with this gun, even though she'd practiced with similar weapons over the years. At close quarters, even under stress, she believed she could fire the weapon and score a hit. Gunfights were not her specialty. Her skills lay elsewhere and likely were the catalyst for this late-night visit. Stuffing a handful of shells into her front right pants pocket, she came back to her feet and continued to move.

She'd drilled for this for years. Dozens of times in the real world, countless times in her head. She never knew who might come for her or how they might find her. But she always knew someone would come. She only hoped she was ready.

The night-light flashed again. A cold sensation raced down her spine. The flickering meant someone had stepped onto a pressure pad on the second floor and they were coming to her room.

She aimed the shotgun at the door.

The knob turned slowly and quietly. Had she been asleep she never would have heard it. She watched as the door swung inward and revealed a big man clad in black standing in the doorway.

In a flash, she saw his hand come up. The night-light's glow glinted on a metallic object in his hand. Without hesitation, her shotgun exploded, twin tongues of flame lashing out from the barrel. The blast hammered the man's midsection, hurled him from the doorway and into a wall opposite her bedroom.

She broke open the shotgun, reloaded.

Her luck was about to run out, that much she knew. She'd just taken out one armed man, probably in part because he'd underestimated her. Or maybe because they'd been ordered to take her alive. Whatever the reason, she guessed things were about to become much worse. They knew she was armed and willing to use a gun. If they were burglars, they'd probably get the hell out. If they were here specifically for her, though, they likely would keep coming for her.

Rounding the door in a low crouch, she gingerly stepped over the body of the first man she'd killed, looked around.

The bulb of a single small lamp burned downstairs, emanating a white glow that quickly was swallowed up by the darkness.

Her ears continued to ring and she forced herself to rely on her eyes as much as possible. She could see shadows shifting along on the walls and guessed others were waiting for her to come down the steps and fight her way out.

Panic started to well up from within. Her knees went rubbery and her chest tightened, making it hard to breathe.

She shook her head. Not happening. She had no idea who they were, or who they worked for, but she guessed her visitors had lost money to her—or more accurately to the Nightingale— meaning they had hurt somebody, maybe many people. Maybe someone like Jessica. An image of her sister—curly blond hair hanging past her shoulders, her stomach curved outward as she entered her third trimester of pregnancy—flashed through her mind. Her breathing slowed and her knees became steady again.

If they'd hurt someone like Jessica, and she'd taken their money, they'd gotten exactly what they deserved.

She crept into a second bedroom. Crossing the floor, she held the shotgun by its pistol grip with one hand and worked the lock on the window with her free hand. She raised the window, which went up about eight inches before it stuck.

She swore through clenched teeth, cast a glance over her shoulder at the door, but saw no one there. With a grunt, she gave the window one last push, but it remained jammed. Leaning the shotgun against the wall, she pushed against the window with both hands. It gave, but with a squeak that sounded like a bomb explosion in the stillness. A moment later, she heard one of the stair steps creaking under someone's weight.

Pulling the .38 from its holster, she spun around and leveled the pistol at the hall. A shadow appeared in the doorway. She snapped off two quick shots. One slug hammered into the molding around the door, splintering the wood. A second drilled into the plasterboard to the right of the door, just a few inches above a light switch. The figure ducked from view.

Several heartbeats ticked by as she remained motionless, the pistol trained on the doorway.

A door slammed shut downstairs with a crack, the unexpected noise startling her body, which was already overloaded with adrenaline. In the distance, she heard sirens. She guessed someone had summoned the police to check out the gunshots. For a normal person, the sound likely would provide some comfort. But she'd relinquished any pretension of normalcy years ago. Her instincts told her to run. Run from the police. Run from the people who'd come for her. Just run like hell and figure the rest out later.

Looping the shotgun over her back, she pushed herself through the window and disappeared into the darkness.

SHUTTING THE DOOR behind her, Davis turned the dead bolt and flicked the wall switch. Fluorescent lights sparked to life and bathed the room in soft white light. A wooden workbench, the surface scarred and blemished, ran the length of one wall. A tool chest, its metal skin scratched and mottled with rust spots, stood in another corner. A compact car, its red paint bleached by exposure to the elements, was parked in the middle of the room.

She shoved her keys into her hip pocket and withdrew one of the cell phones from her belt pack. With her thumb, she punched through a group of numbers, put the phone to her ear and listened as it dialed through a series of cutouts. She noticed her hands starting to shake, immediately felt her face flush.

It's just adrenaline, she told herself. You've been through hell. It's catching up with you. Ignore it.

After two rings, someone picked up on the other end.

"Yes?" It was Maxine.

"Good to hear your voice."

"You okay?"

"All things considered."

"What happened?"

"Someone came after me tonight."

"Who?" Maxine asked, concern evident in her voice.

"I'm not sure. There were at least two people."

"They still after you?"

"Not those two."

"Does that mean what I think it means?"

"Yes."

"Let me ask again—are you okay?"

"No, but it needed to be done," she replied. She gave a small shrug even though Maxine couldn't see her.

"I'm sure it needed to be done. I'm glad you weren't hurt."

Davis said nothing.

"What's your next move?"

"Get out of here," Davis replied.

"And go where?"

"Tell you when I get there."

"You don't know? Or you don't want me to know?"

"The latter."

"Thanks."

"It's not like that. Someone's looking for me. They found me. Who knows what else they know—about me, the network, you. I need to disappear. It's probably better that no one knows where I am."

"I understand," Maxine replied, her tone telegraphing that she didn't understand.

"Do me a favor."

"Of course."

"I had to leave in a hurry. Call Nigel. Ask him to do a remote wipe of my systems. Please. I'll also need some equipment. Cell phone—the usual stuff. Need to replace what I lost."

"Consider it done. What else?"

"Nothing. Yet. I'll be in touch."

Davis ended the call and stuffed the phone back into her belt pack. She shut her eyes, rubbed her temples with the first two fingers of each hand. An image flashed across her mind, the first man she'd gunned down, body thrust back by the shotgun blast, his midsection ripped open. Her eyes snapped wide open and she covered her mouth with her hand. My God, she thought, I killed two people on this night, murdered them. A heaviness settled over her, dragged her to her knees. She hung her head, covered her face with her hands and sobbed.

1

Mack Bolan, a.k.a. the Executioner, rolled into the War Room at Stony Man Farm.

He wore blue denim jeans, a black turtleneck and black leather tennis shoes. Gathered around the room were Hal Brognola, Director of the Justice Department's Special Operations Group, Barb Price, Stony Man Farm's mission controller, and Aaron the "Bear" Kurtzman, the head of the Farm's cyber team. Brognola, shirt sleeves rolled up almost to his elbows, the top button of his dress shirt undone and his tie pulled loose, was seated at the head of the briefing table. Kurtzman sat to Brognola's right, in his motorized wheelchair, a laptop computer open on the table in front of him. Price, her honey-blond hair pulled into a ponytail, saw Bolan first and flashed him a smile.

"Welcome back, Striker," she said. "It's good to have you back."

Bolan nodded. "I have a feeling I won't be here long. Am I right?"

"Very perceptive, Striker," Brognola said. "As always, the choice is yours. But I think you'll want a piece of the action on this, once you hear about it."

The big Fed gestured at one of the high-backed chairs that ringed the table and Bolan settled into the nearest one. He set a brushed-steel travel mug filled with coffee on the table.

Kurtzman studied the cup for a couple of moments before giving Bolan a puzzled look.

"What's that?"

"Coffee, last I checked."

"I can see it's coffee."

"Then why ask?"

Kurtzman gestured with a nod at the drip coffeemaker that stood on a nearby counter.

"I made coffee."

"I know."

"You could have had some."

"True."

The creases in Kurtzman's forehead deepened.

"But you didn't want my coffee."

"I didn't say that."

"You didn't have to."

"I just wanted this coffee, that's all."

"Because it's better than mine."

"I just wanted this coffee," Bolan said. "That's all."

Brognola cleared his throat. "Seriously, I could listen to you clowns do this all day. But if you'll indulge me."

Kurtzman scowled. "This isn't over," he said, jabbing at the air between them with his forefinger.

Bolan nodded and gulped some coffee from his mug.

"Sorry to call you back in, Striker. Especially on the heels of another mission. But I wanted to give you first crack at this one."

"I'm listening."

Brognola pulled an unlit cigar from his mouth, set it in an ashtray.

"You ever heard of the Nightingale?"

"Assuming you don't mean Florence or the bird, I'd have to say no."

"You're right. I don't mean either of them. It's a person, maybe several persons—we've not been able to nail it down. But there's someone out there who's been ripping people off for years, stealing money from their bank accounts."

"White-collar cyber crime? Not exactly my area."

"Agreed," Brognola said. "But it's not what you think. This— well, let's assume it's one person for the sake of argument—this individual targets a lot of the same people you do. Mobsters, terrorists, arms smugglers, even heads of corrupt states."

"Steals their money?"

Brognola nodded. "Right from under their noses. He, she, whatever, is very good at this, too. Best we can tell the Nightingale steals pretty much with impunity."

"From some very deserving people," Bolan said. "Sorry, Hal, still trying to see how this applies to me."

"Getting there, Striker. We don't know what this individual does with the money. Rumor has it he or she has passed some of it along to crime victims, through a series of cutouts."

"An altruistic thief," Bolan said.

"Altruism or a big middle finger to her victims," Brognola said, "we're not really sure. Maybe both. Psychologists at Langley did a work-up and believe it's as much as anything a way to salve this person's guilt."

"Guilt for?"

"For stealing," Price answered.

"From scum," Bolan countered. "Bad people."

Price shrugged. "Good people, bad people. If you're raised not to steal, you're going to feel bad about it. Doesn't matter if you know in your heart you're doing the right thing. You're still going to feel guilty."

Bolan nodded his understanding. In his War Everlasting, he'd tried to maintain a few basic rules. Don't harm police, even crooked ones. Don't put innocent bystanders in harm's way, even if it means letting a target escape. These rules had helped him maintain his humanity even when surrounded by hellfire and chaos. Though he's killed countless times, he takes no joy from it.

"I can understand that," he said.

"Thought you could," Price replied.

"So, again, what does this have to do with me? And Stony Man Farm, for that matter?"

"We're not one hundred percent sure ourselves. But we think the Nightingale may be in trouble," Price said.

"Not that I'm unsympathetic," Bolan said, "but there are a lot of people in the world who are in trouble."

"We, that being the United States, have been tracking this person for a couple of years," Brognola said, "ever since we confirmed their existence really. At first, we only caught small whiffs. Our intelligence agencies would hear a drug kingpin or a terrorist bitching because a bank account came up empty. The first few times, we wrote it off. We figured they were getting ripped off the old-fashioned way, either through an inside job or by a rival. The more analysts put the pieces together, though, the clearer it became that someone was picking their pockets." A smile played on his lips. "And that someone was getting away with it."

"How much did they get away with?"

Brognola shrugged. "It's hard to say. Estimates run into the tens of millions of dollars. But they're just that, estimates. A lot of the countries where the thefts occurred, well, the record keeping is for shit. And in Switzerland and some of the Caribbean countries? Not exactly bastions of transparency."

Bolan looked at Kurtzman and cocked an eyebrow. "Since when has that stopped you?"

"I'm working on it," Kurtzman said. "I'm working on it."

The Executioner turned back to Price.

"You said this person—"

"Or persons," she said.

"—or persons, could be in trouble. What makes you think that?"

Brognola pushed a thin stack of photos across the table to Bolan. The big American picked up the pile and studied the one on top. It was a picture of a man sprawled on the floor. His face was so pale from blood loss it seemed to glow. Dead eyes stared skyward. The flesh of his torso was shredded. The soldier glanced up at Brognola.

"Bear mauling?"

"Shotgun blast, smart-ass," Brognola said. "Very close range. Gutted the stupid bastard."

Nodding, Bolan peeled the photo from the stack, set it face-down on the table and studied the next one. The next photo depicted a man laying in a hallway, his chest torn open. He glanced up at Brognola.

"Shotgun?"

"Bravo, Columbo. These two were found in a London residence, which based on the little evidence left behind, we think may have most recently been inhabited by Nightingale."

"Any IDs on them?"

"Russian, both of them," Brognola said. "The names are in the case file. Frankly, they're inconsequential. Couple of hired hands. Interpol had listed them as suspects in a couple of murders, one in France, a second in the Netherlands. Not a couple of Boy Scouts. But they're hardly supervillains."

"But you don't know who they're working for?"

Brognola shook his head.

"I'll get to that. But, in short, we believe it's someone Nightingale stole from. From what we've been able to scrape together, they flew into London a couple of days ago. Bought their airline tickets under false names, with fake credit cards. Nothing in their luggage was of any use. If they hadn't been busted for petty crimes along the way, it's possible we never would have made them."

"They leave anything behind?"

"Couple of cell phones. The London authorities are tracking them. We'll see how far it takes them. Their weapons, obviously. Night-vision goggles. A rental car."

"Most likely they didn't fly into London with all that stuff," Bolan said. "They must have had someone on the ground supplying them."

"We thought of that," Brognola said. "Solid theory. We don't have the intel to back it up, though. But we have someone working that angle."

"That someone is?"

"David McCarter."

"McCarter's in London? My apologies to the queen."

Brognola grinned. "David was already over there, buying a Jaguar that had been buried under some tarps in a garage somewhere. We thought it might help having someone on the ground to act as—" Brognola made quotation marks with his fingers "—a liaison between MI5, Scotland Yard and the U.S."

"God help us."

"Yeah, we needed a diplomat, but we got McCarter. Imagine."

"The Brits will appreciate his deft touch."

"Look," Brognola said, "here's the upshot of all this. As you can imagine, the U.S. government finds itself in a unique position here. Officially, the government doesn't condone vigilantes. We don't condone stealing money from people, even if they're criminals and terrorists, unless it's part of a sanctioned intelligence operation."

"There's a 'but' coming."

Brognola downed some coffee and nodded. "Absolutely. What this person has accomplished is pretty damn amazing. As best we know, she or he has no governments backing her."

"Which means no government-imposed constraints."

"As I said, what Nightingale has been able to accomplish is nothing short of amazing," Brognola said. "This person has acquired account numbers and pieced together complex financial networks. He or she knows lots of things, and we want to know how."

Bolan's eyes narrowed and he leaned forward. "Look, if you want someone to plug a leak."

"Hardly," Brognola replied, shaking his head vigorously. "Frankly, we want to recruit this person. Nightingale could fill in gaps in our knowledge. There's a place for those skills."

"Off the books, of course," Price interjected. "But we can offer full legal protection, a new identity, the works."

"What leads do we have?" Bolan asked.

Kurtzman gestured at the stack of photos in Bolan's hand.

"Look through those," he said, "stop when you find a picture of a white-haired guy."

Bolan found a close-up of a round-faced man with pink cheeks, pale green eyes and white hair trimmed down to stubble. He studied the photo for a couple of seconds, then tossed it, face up, on the tabletop. "This the guy?"

"That'd be him," Kurtzman said. "His name is Jonathan Salis-

bury. He's British by birth, but moved to the United States in
the early 1970s and eventually became a citizen. Did a lot of
computer work for the Pentagon, all highly classified. Guy was
a genius."

"Was?"

"He's dead," Kurtzman said. "Poor bastard asphyxiated himself in a garage. Neighbors found him in the car while it still was
running. Hadn't been dead long. I have a file I'll give you with
some clips about him. It was big news in the Beltway when he
died."

"I've never heard of him. He famous in computer circles?"

"More like infamous," Kurtzman said. "Technically, he was
in deep shit with the Feds."

Bolan sipped his coffee. "Isn't that like being a little pregnant?"

"I knew the guy," Kurtzman said. "We weren't friends, but I
knew him. I knew his work. To say he was brilliant would be an
understatement. His depth of knowledge when it came to computers and cybersecurity was nearly unmatched."

"Except by you."

"There are maybe three dozen people with this guy's chops.
Me and thirty-five others." Kurtzman allowed himself a grin,
though it faded almost immediately. "That said, the guy was
branded a traitor."

"Because?"

"He tapped into the Defense Intelligence Agency's computers, dug up some records on a Russian guy, Mikhail Yezhov, and
passed it along."

"Passed it along to whom?"

Kurtzman shrugged. "Nobody knows for sure," he said.

"That's a pretty big deal."

"Sure," Kurtzman said. "I'm not saying otherwise. I'm not
suggesting otherwise. But there were extenuating circumstances.
His wife was killed. Not by Yezhov, but a couple of his shooters.
At least that was the working theory of the Russian investigators.
Not a far-fetched theory, either. But the Russians didn't want to
go after Yezhov, so they let the whole thing go. Salisbury's wife

was a criminal justice professor and taught at Georgetown University. She'd written a couple of papers on Yezhov's network and then she turned up dead."

"The Justice Department tried to get the Russians off the dime on this thing," Brognola added, "but they wouldn't budge. Apparently, Yezhov rates top-level protection in his country."

"You think Salisbury got pissed off enough to steal information?" Bolan asked.

"And pass it along to Nightingale? Yeah, I do. That's the theory. And our two dead friends have links to Yezhov, too."

"Clearly," Brognola said, "we think Salisbury killed himself. The forensic evidence says so. His coworkers and friends confirmed that he was despondent after his wife's murder. That he couldn't at least get a little closure likely only made things worse."

"So he takes matters into his own hands," Bolan said. "He gets caught and loses his security clearance and his reputation. And kills himself."

"Right," Brognola said.

"A month before the ceiling fell in on the guy, he took a trip to London," Kurtzman said. "We're assuming he took the intelligence he stole to England and passed it to someone else."

"But we don't know who for sure?" Bolan asked.

"No," Kurtzman said, "we don't. But we are hedging our bets that it was Nightingale. Yezhov likely sent these two thugs out to exact a little revenge, but they obviously underestimated Nightingale's skill."

"Will you take the assignment, Striker?" Brognola asked.

"What if I find Nightingale and he or she tells me to go to hell?"

"Then they do," Brognola said. "Technically, the Nightingale is a fugitive. But you're not a cop. Besides, I am guessing you have no interest in strong-arming someone just because Washington wants a chat with them."

"Good guess."

"You can say no," Brognola said.

Bolan nodded. He'd always kept an arm's-length relationship

with the federal government and could turn down assignments that came his way. But his gut told him this one was important. He agreed to take it.

2

Mikhail Yezhov wanted to smash something.

The man who stood before him, armpits of his shirt darkened with perspiration, breathing audible, seemed to sense it. Yezhov, fists clenched, a deep scarlet coloring his neck, circled the man, staring at him. The occasional flinch, or flicker of fear in the man's eyes, caused a warm sense of satisfaction to well up inside Yezhov.

Decked out in a five-thousand-dollar suit, surrounded by shelves of leather-bound books, and mahogany wood-paneled walls, Yezhov looked like a Wall Street investment banker or a shipping magnate. He was neither. Though he had once posed as a stockbroker in London as an agent with Soviet intelligence during the waning days of the Cold War. But his background wasn't in business; he'd been a Soviet soldier and a military intelligence officer during his brief career. Once the Communist state went belly up, he'd moved into the private sector, where he could use his talents as a spy to whip up mayhem for his clients against their competitors. He always guaranteed results and, on the rare occasions when he couldn't deliver, it made him see red.

Like the present.

Like Yezhov, the man who stood before him was Russian. That was where the similarities ended as far as Yezhov was concerned. This foot soldier—was his name Josef or Dmitri?—had a slight frame compared to Yezhov's bulk, big eyes that made him look surprised even in the calmest moments and acne that would embarrass a fourteen-year-old boy. His suit jacket hung limply from his narrow shoulders and beads of sweat had formed on his upper lip. All this only intensified his air of akwardness, in Yezhov's opinion. When the man swallowed, his Adam's apple popped audibly in the deathly quiet room.

Yezhov moved in front of the man, stopped circling. He pinned the guy under his gaze.

"What now?"

"Our sources in Scotland Yard said they identified the two bodies," the man said.

"Hardly a surprise."

"Sir?"

"You hired known criminals to kill this woman. Neither was high-profile, but both had criminal records. It's no surprise the police identified them. It was only a matter of time."

The man opened his mouth to protest, apparently thought better of it, and slammed his jaw shut.

"Now, we have two corpses and a home that has been shot all to hell."

"Yes."

"And the woman lives."

"Yes, she does."

"And we have no idea where she is."

The man paused, studied his black wingtip shoes for a couple of seconds before nodding in agreement.

"We have people looking for her," he said. "It's only a matter of time—"

"Before you mess this up even more."

The man replied, but Yezhov didn't bother to listen. He turned and saw his own reflection in a mirror that ran the length of the wall behind his desk. The rectangular mirror stretched from about the middle of the wall up to a foot short of the ceiling. It was one-way glass, on the other side of which was a small room packed with a console that controlled an array of audio and visual recording equipment. While he didn't record every meeting, this one included, the setup came in handy when he gathered with high-level business executives and government officials from Russia and other countries, allowing him to gather blackmail material on the participants. As he'd said in rare unguarded moments, he had no business partners, only future victims.

Yezhov saw plenty in his reflection to admire. Though he stood a couple of inches below six feet, he was broad in the chest and shoulders, straining the fabric of his shirt. Arms crossed over his chest were thick, corded with muscles created with an exacting exercise regiment and anabolic steroids. His head was shaved clean. Small hazel-colored eyes, set far apart, peered out from his wide face, and were separated by a large nose that had been broken twice, once in combat and once in a bar fight.

For some reason, the annoying buzz of the other man's words reached Yezhov, prompted him to turn back around and face the man.

"We'll find her," he said.

"No," Yezhov said, shaking his head, "*we'll* find her. You'll have no part in this."

Surprise registered on the other man's face.

"Sir?"

"You're done."

"But—"

"But nothing. You had a location. You had a name. You had money, my fucking money. You fucked it up. You're done."

The man opened his mouth to speak. Yezhov silenced him with a gesture.

"Shut. The. Fuck. Up," he said. "This was a simple operation. A snatch-and-grab. One woman. The bitch was a banker, not a soldier. You hired two criminals, neither of whom apparently was up to the challenge." He came around the desk and put himself between it and the other man. "I sent you to solve a problem, one fucking problem. Instead, you created more for me."

"Sir…" the man began.

Yezhov, who'd been resting his backside against the edge of the desktop, arms hanging loose at his sides, made his move. His arms snaked out. The man flinched, but had no time to move before Yezhov's fingers encircled his throat, thumbs levering down on the man's windpipe. A pitiful gurgle escaped the man's lips and he brought up his own hands, grabbed at Yezhov's forearms. For a skinny man, his grip was surprisingly strong, Yezhov thought. Yezhov rewarded the man's efforts by pressing harder against his throat. More seconds passed before the man's body went limp. When Yezhov finally was satisfied that his failed employee was dead, he released his grip and let the man's limp body strike the floor with a thump in a boneless heap.

Yezhov turned and motioned for one of his guards to step forward. That guard, a combat veteran who'd killed Chechen militants without fear or conscience, hesitated pleased Yezhov. The Russian leader pointed at the body lying on the floor.

"Get that thing out of here," he said.

The man nodded. Stepping forward, he knelt next to the corpse and raised the dead man's torso at an angle, rested it against a bent knee. Grabbing the dead man from under his arms, the guard stood and dragged the limp form from the room.

"Lovely," Yezhov muttered under his breath as he watched the whole thing.

A glance at the other guards situated around the room told Yezhov they were trying hard not to look at him, making a show at staring into their drinks or at one of the flat-screen televisions positioned throughout the room. That they were scared made him feel all the more powerful. But, he told himself, it wasn't just about venting his anger. He wanted to teach these bastards a lesson. The price of failure in his organization was steep. And in his latest venture, with its high stakes, failure needed to be dealt with quickly and severely, not just because it made him feel good, but as a practical matter. Everyone needed to function at the highest levels possible.

Turning, he went back to his desk and hoisted the receiver on a secure telephone that stood there. Going from memory, he punched in a series of numbers. After a couple of seconds, it began ringing, his impatience growing with each ring. Finally, a familiar voice answered.

"What?" the man rasped.

"It's me."

A couple of seconds passed. "Okay."

"I have a job for you."

"A job for me?" Dmitri Mikoyan's voice sounded incredulous. "Go to hell."

"Look, you ungrateful—"

"Ungrateful? Remember Tajikistan? You almost got me killed ten times over. I'm grateful to be away from you."

"I need you to run an operation," Yezhov said. Mikoyan said nothing, but Yezhov heard him clucking his tongue on the other end of the connection. From experience, Yezhov knew that sound meant Mikoyan was thinking. Yezhov wasn't even sure whether the other man even was aware of the noise, the habit.

"How much money?" Mikoyan asked.

"Don't you want to hear the job first?"

"No. I know you. If you called me, it's a crap job. The details don't matter because the job will suck no matter what. So tell me about the money first and I'll decide whether it's worth my time."

"Trust me, it is."

"What is it the Americans say? Money talks. Bullshit walks. Give me numbers."

Yezhov said an amount, twice Mikoyan's usual fee.

Mikoyan laughed. "What am I? A bag lady? That is crap pay!"

"It's also my only offer."

More tongue clucking sounded from the other end of the line. "Okay, I'll take it."

"I need you to snatch someone—a woman."

"Sounds horribly complicated," Mikoyan said, sarcasm evident in his voice.

"You've heard of the Nightingale?"

"Nightingale? Sure, I've heard the stories. Total bullshit. No one can steal all that money and get away with it."

"It's not bullshit."

"Sure it is," Mikoyan insisted. "It's a story some crooked accountant cooked up after he embezzled money from the wrong guy. Did it to save his own ass. Don't tell me you've bought in to this fairy tale."

"I have."

"Please—"

"She stole from me."

"How much?"

"It doesn't matter. It was a lot. The point is, she stole from me. I can't tolerate that."

"You want the money back."

Yezhov shrugged even though the other man couldn't see him. "I have little hope that will happen."

"Why?"

"Think about it. You think she has dollars sitting around in suitcases somewhere? My guess is she takes what she steals, splits it into a dozen or so accounts and makes it all disappear. The last thing she wants is for someone to track her or take what she has stolen."

"Okay, you don't want the money. What do you want?"

"I do want the money—I just don't have much hope I'll get it back."

"Fair enough."

"I want her. I want her alive, Dmitri. I want to kill her with my bare hands."

"To send a message."

"Yes."

"Consider it done."

"I sent two other men to do it. Or, more to the point, one of my employees sent two men." Yezhov glanced at the spot on the carpet where the recently removed corpse had fallen. "Make that a former employee. Anyway, they both ended up dead."

"Should've called me first."

"Maybe. I'll send a courier with more information."

The line went dead and Yezhov slammed down the phone.

A single, soft knock sounded against his office door. He looked up in time to see the door swing open and a woman enter. As always, her fire-red hair, which cascaded past her shoulders, caught his attention first, followed by her jade-green eyes. Her full lips spread into a wide smile, lips parting enough to expose even white teeth.

"Tatania," he said, returning the smile. "Can I get you a drink?"

"Yes," Tatania Sizova said.

Crossing the room, she walked to him, reached up and kissed him lightly on the cheek. Stepping back, she eased herself into one of the wingback chairs that stood in front of Yezhov's desk. Crossing her legs, she placed her folded hands into her lap.

Yezhov looked at his guards and dismissed them with a nod. One by one, they filed from the room. He finished making her drink—a gin and tonic—and handed it to her.

She thanked him for the beverage and, looking at him over its rim, sampled it.

"Lovely," she said.

"Good."

"I've seen little of you this week. You've been up early and working late into the night."

He shrugged. "It's nothing."

"It's the woman," Sizova replied.

He glared at her. If she felt threatened, though, she didn't let it show. Instead, she sipped from the gin and tonic again, then set it on a small table.

"You're obsessed with the woman," she said. "She's pissed you off."

"Nonsense! There's no room for that in my operation. Stakes are too high."

"Of course."

Yezhov detected something in her voice.

"What?" he asked.

"I'm worried, that's all."

"Worried? About?"

"You."

"I'm fine."

"Are you? You're focused on this woman. We're in the middle of something so much larger and you are worried about her, about revenge."

"I'm focused on the mission."

"The mission doesn't include chasing shadows or drawing attention to us with ham-handed kidnapping attempts."

"Don't tell me what the mission is," he said, an edge creeping into his voice.

Sizova sat back in her chair, as though stung. Her lips pressed together in an angry line and her eyes narrowed. Yezhov had seen the look before and knew he had crossed a line. He also was angry enough not to care.

"Don't speak to me like that," she said.

"Don't tell me how to run my operation," he said. "I have this under control."

Her angry look turned to one of mild amusement.

"I can tell," she said.

He fought the urge to come out of his chair and hit the woman. Experience told him not to. Sizova, outwardly gorgeous and delicate, had been trained since her teen years in the dark arts of hand-to-hand combat, as well as with weapons. Even if he did take her, he'd pay a price for his victory—a lost eye or an ear torn from the side of his head. That was the best-case scenario.

Yezhov exhaled.

"I have this under control," he repeated. "Taking her out isn't an aside from our mission—it's a major piece of our mission."

Her expression softened.

"What do you mean?"

Yezhov stood up and walked to the small bar. Grabbing a clear glass tumbler, he turned it over and reached for the vodka.

"What do I mean?" he said, unscrewing the bottle's cap. "I mean, she knows. Or she *will* know what we're up to."

"Stop being so damned cryptic!" she said.

Satisfied with the amount he had poured into his glass, he put the top back on the bottle and set it aside. Picking up the drink, her turned and looked at her.

"I mean she knows. She knows more than my fucking bank balance. When she hacked into our system, she stole all kinds of information."

Sizova had paled slightly.

"Our deal," she said.

"Yes, our deal," he said. "The Sentry project, the antisatellite technology—she has that information."

"Maybe she hasn't seen it."

Yezhov shrugged. "Maybe, maybe not. She stole tons of data.

It's possible she hasn't had time to look through it yet. But it's also likely she has. At some point, she will comb through all of it, exploit the information for further attacks on us. Regardless, we have to proceed as if she knows."

"Meaning—"

"Meaning we have to kill her. And anyone who's helping her. But first we must find her. Luckily, I have a plan for that."

3

Bolan and McCarter met outside the headquarters of MI5, Britain's domestic intelligence agency. The fox-faced Briton, a Coke in his grip, was leaning against an iron railing and staring out at the Thames River, swollen from a recent rain. The Executioner noticed his old friend wore a black trench coat and a red necktie that occasionally lashed out from beneath the coat. A black leather valise stood on the concrete next to McCarter's leg.

Seeing Bolan from the corner of his eye, McCarter turned and shot the Executioner a lopsided grin and a small wave.

"Welcome to paradise, Yank," he said.

"Glad to be home?" Bolan asked.

McCarter shrugged. "Longer I'm away, the less it feels like home. Good to be here, though. I did get a hell of a deal on a Jaguar. Sweet little black number."

"Love to see it."

"See it from a distance, if it's all the same," McCarter said. "The cars you touch tend to end up pocked with bullet holes or blown to smithereens. I'd at least like to race this one once or twice before it ends up in the scrap heap."

"Fair enough," Bolan said, a smile ghosting his lips. "Our friends at MI5 playing nice?"

"Nice as can be expected, considering I just swooped in from across the pond and asked to see the family jewels. The bloke here, Damon Blair, seems decent enough. Balked a little at first, but got on board once he found out we have some heavyweights behind us."

Bolan nodded. "Good, let's go see what he has to say."

Blair's office was on the top floor of Thames House and had a window that overlooked the river. Blair was a small man, with straw-blond hair that was unkempt, a wide nose and large ears.

Bolan identified himself under his oft-used alias, Matt Cooper. Blair gestured for the two men to sit.

Bolan lowered himself into a chair that stood in front of Blair's desk. McCarter took the seat next to him. Leaning forward, Blair laced his fingers together and set them on the desktop.

"Welcome to our fair city, Mr. Cooper," Blair said.

"Matt," Bolan replied.

"David says you're looking for information."

Bolan nodded.

"You want information on the Nightingale."

Bolan nodded again.

"Man of few words, eh?" Blair said. "Well, not sure what I can offer you. As you can understand, we can't—and I won't—tell you specific sources."

"Sure."

"And the Americans probably have a lot of the same raw intelligence on this as we do. So I'm not sure what I have to add."

Bolan crossed his legs, right ankle balanced on left knee.

"Fair question," the big American said. "And, you're right, our two countries probably have a lot of the same information, since we share so much. But you have two advantages. One, you've been following this individual for—what?—a couple of years now. And, two, you actually are on the ground. The shootings happened in Bayswater, just a stone's throw from here. I'm guessing you've seen all the latest information on the shooting, including any police reports and other intelligence gathered. You know the area. You might have some insights into Nightingale's behavior that a guy like me, someone who just parachuted into town, would miss entirely."

Blair grinned. "So you can speak, eh? Okay, fair enough. What questions can I field for you two?"

The Executioner noticed the other man didn't promise to actually answer the questions, but let it slide.

"What's your take on the Nightingale?" Bolan asked.

Leaning back in his chair, Blair glanced at the ceiling and rubbed absently at his throat for a moment, apparently collecting his thoughts.

"*She*—our psychologists believe she's a woman—she's lost something. More likely she's lost someone, maybe even several people, and she's enraged. Probably so enraged she no longer feels or notices it. It's like an arthritic joint. Bugs you all the time, affects how you move, maybe your choice in activities and lifestyle. But you've become so accustomed to it, you barely pay attention to it. Or you only do so on a limited basis."

"I don't buy it," McCarter said. "How can someone be that bloody angry and not know it?"

"Pot meet kettle," Blair said

"Don't put me on the shrink's couch," McCarter growled.

"Above my pay grade."

"She's angry," Bolan interjected.

"Enraged. Enraged, but conflicted. She obviously feels some guilt over what she does. That means she's going against her grain by stealing."

"Our analysts guessed the same thing," the Executioner added.

Blair nodded. "That's all low-hanging fruit. The real question is what does it all mean? And what is it about her that makes her handle her anger this way? A lot of people have bad things happen to them, things that change their lives and their perspectives. But this made her, well, a little daft. Not insane in the classic sense, mind you, but it knocked her off course. Our shrinks believe underneath all the rage and activity lies a lot of guilt."

"For?"

"Whoever got hurt, she probably feels—or felt—responsible for them. Not for the action that hurt them, but for not being there to save that person. Maybe even for not being killed, too."

"You mean survivor guilt," Bolan asked.

"Sure. And a little bit of that is normal, especially with a tragedy. But this—starting a whole new life, going underground—

smacks of someone trying to atone for something. Not just wondering why a bullet or a bomb didn't take them instead. But really trying to atone for something done or, hell, not done for that matter."

"That being?" McCarter asked.

Blair shrugged. "Hell if I know."

"Thanks for crystallizing it, lad," McCarter said.

Blair's neck and cheeks turned scarlet. "Sorry, didn't realize I was supposed to do all your damn thinking for you."

Uncrossing his legs, Bolan leaned forward.

"You're a smart guy," Bolan said, his voice even. "You have a theory."

"Lots of theories. That's how I spend my days, collecting information and spouting theories. When it comes to this young lady, though, it seems pretty damned easy actually."

Bolan gave what he hoped was an encouraging nod. Apparently it worked.

"If we have traced her history back far enough—and it's a big bloody 'if'—her first two strikes occurred less than five years ago. Hit the money men for al Qaeda in Mesopotamia, the Iraqi branch. Pretty nice piece of work, that. From what we know their IT crew came straight from Saddam's government, a Sunni who studied computer science at Oxford. Once we knocked Saddam out of power, this guy suddenly found himself out of a job, got pissed off and joined al Qaeda. Lots of Sunnis did that in those days."

"Got a name?" McCarter asked.

"He does," Blair replied. "Khallad Mukhtar. Not that it matters. The Americans took him out years ago. Hit his car with a Hellfire missile while he was tooling 'round Tikrit. Took out three other al Qaeda guys, his security detail, in the process."

"Good show, that one," McCarter said.

"Indeed. But here's my point, Nightingale already hit him months before that. She also hit two guys in London, a couple of Saudis, couple of fire breathers. They collected all kinds of money from sympathizers, not just in the Middle East, but also

Europe, and funneled it back to al Qaeda's operations in Iraq and Saudi Arabia. One of those assholes got deported back to his own country. Saudis put him into a government-sponsored rehabilitation program. When he reappeared six months later, he was a changed man, denounced al Qaeda and the Jihad."

"A real beacon of light," McCarter said. He took a swig from his Coke and swallowed loudly.

"An organic change of heart to be sure," Blair said, allowing himself a dour smile.

"So she went after Islamists from Iraq," Bolan said. "You thinking she's related to a soldier killed in Iraq?"

"That was my original thought," Blair said. "But that didn't sit well with me. Not entirely, anyway."

"Because?"

"Originally, it was a gut feeling. But I started piecing this thing together more and found another common strand between our first targets."

Turning slightly in his chair, the analyst's left hand disappeared below the desktop and the soldier heard a drawer being pulled open. Blair hummed and Bolan heard papers rustling. When Blair's hand came back into view, he had a photograph and a couple of newspaper clippings in his hand. He tossed the items on the desk. Bolan and McCarter leaned forward and studied the items.

The picture was a still photo of carnage. The crumpled remains of a train car on its side, its silver skin scorched black, the interior belching oily smoke. It apparently had been ripped from between two other cars and thrown from the tracks. The soldier saw firefighters armed with hoses dousing the car with water. An officer from London's Metropolitan Police pointed at something unseen, mouth open in a yell, while two other officers ushered civilians away from the wreckage.

Blair smoothed down one of the rumpled newspaper clippings with his palm, pushed it forward so the Stony Man warriors could read it.

"I know I could have printed it out from the internet," he said, "but I'm still partial to the newsprint-and-ink version."

Bolan nodded, but focused his attention on the clipping.

Terror Bombing Kills Seven

Seven passengers were killed—including a pregnant woman on holiday—and three others were injured when a bomb planted by an Islamic militant group tore through a train car's interior.

The dead also included four London residents, a French tourist and another American, a man believed to be the husband of the pregnant woman killed in Sunday's explosion, authorities said.

In a statement sent to news organizations, a group of Islamic militants with ties to al Qaeda in Iraq claimed responsibility for the bombing. The act was meant as a protest against the presence of British troops in Iraq, according to the statement.

Bolan scanned through the rest of the article, but found few other details useful to his search. It mostly contained eyewitness statements and comments from police and politicians vowing to hunt down those responsible.

Blair spread out a second article on the desk. Between the headline and the story, Bolan saw the photos of seven individuals lined up.

With his index finger, Blair tapped the picture of a young woman. The photo portrayed her from the shoulders up. Her hair was blond and her mouth was turned up in a warm smile.

"That's the American. Name's Jessica Harrison. Beautiful young woman. According to a *New York Times* profile that ran at the time, she was six months pregnant. Her husband, Jeremy, was fresh from foreign-service officer school and was stationed at the London embassy. He'd been in the country four months before he was killed. She arrived that day. They were on their way from Heathrow to the U.S. embassy compound. Diplomatic cables and other information from your government pretty much confirmed the information in the *Times* piece."

It struck Bolan that the analyst was drawing details completely from memory.

"You've spent a lot of time on this," the soldier said.

Blair gave him a lopsided grin. "Shows, doesn't it? Normal people have hobbies or, better yet, girlfriends. Anyway, I thought for sure this woman was the key. See, she had a twin sister, Jennifer Davis—Davis was the dead woman's maiden name. Her sister worked for a couple of major U.S. banks. Really understood the nuts and bolts of financial transactions. And did I mention she oversaw information security at another point in her career?"

"Happy coincidence," McCarter muttered.

"Smart woman, obviously. Quite lovely, too, though more serious than her sister, judging by the photos I've seen."

"So she went underground?" Bolan asked.

"In a manner of speaking," Blair said. "She's dead."

"Dead?" Bolan leaned forward.

"Very much so. As I said, she was my favorite guess for the Nightingale when I first started poring over all this stuff. But circumstances have forced me to change my mind."

"'Circumstance' being that she's dead," the Executioner said.

Blair nodded. "Seems a logical conclusion to draw, doesn't it? It's not likely she faked her own death and just fell off the grid. I mean, right? Who does that?"

Bolan said nothing. In the waning days of his war on the Mafia, he'd done just that, allegedly dying after a bomb destroyed his war wagon. When that ruse fell apart, he'd been forced to stand trial for the blood spilled in his War Everlasting. Ultimately, he'd "died" a second and, as far as the public was concerned, final time. This time it had stuck, but that was partly because of his experiences as a soldier and the help of the White House and Stony Man Farm.

Presumably, this young woman had none of those resources at hand, he told himself.

"She died in a house explosion," Blair said. "It was six months after her sister died. The local fire department blamed it on a gas leak. Neighbors saw her walk in after work. An hour later, an explosion tears through the house, incinerates the damn thing."

"They thought it was suicide," Bolan said.

"According to her coworkers and family, she collapsed when

her sister died, took a month off work to recover from the shock. When she finally did come back, people said she'd changed. She was sullen, depressed and withdrawn."

"No surprise," McCarter said.

"Agreed. But as time went on, according to the interviews I saw, she got worse rather than better. Since her sister was lost in a terrorist attack, the authorities gave the case a hard look before they closed it, but they found no signs of foul play. She could have died from an accident, which seems plausible. She'd called the gas company to the house at least once about a month before the explosion to report the smell of gas. Or she gave up and killed herself."

Bolan nodded. "If she's dead, why tell us all this?"

"More to illustrate a point," Blair said. "Jennifer Davis fits the profile pretty well. So do a couple of other women. They didn't check out, either, for various reasons. If you're trying to find the Nightingale, it won't be easy. That's really the point I am trying to make here. You're chasing a ghost."

They spent the next hour going through the other information Blair had, including other suspects who'd turned out to be false leads. The Stony Man warriors thanked Blair for his help and left Thames House, along with a flood of civil servants heading out for lunch.

"Fun to yank his chain, but he seems like a good enough lad," McCarter said. "Not much help, though. Sorry for dragging you out here."

"It's been a long flight," Bolan said. "Let's see if Kurtzman dug up anything in the meantime."

AFTER HIS VISITORS left, Blair forced himself to sit in his office and, for an excruciating twenty-two minutes, pretended to work. Finally, he grabbed his sack lunch from his bottom desk drawer, grabbed his windbreaker from a hook on the wall and headed out the door.

A nervous flutter in his stomach nagged at him and, as he made his way through the corridors of Thames House, he felt as though all eyes rested upon him. He bought a foam cup filled with hot tea from a street vendor and walked a few blocks from MI5's headquarters, where he bought a couple of newspapers from a newsstand.

Though he tried to look nonchalant about it, he surveyed the streets for any signs he'd been followed. He saw nothing amiss, but knew that meant absolutely zero. He wasn't a trained field operative. Though he understood surveillance and countersurveillance techniques and principles, he hadn't applied them in the real world. Said other ways, he was out of his element, over his head or any other clichés one wanted to apply.

Folding the newspapers in half, he put them under his arm and continued on two more blocks to a small municipal park. With the edge of the folded newspapers, he brushed some leaves and other debris from a wrought-iron bench. He seated himself on the bench, drew his tuna sandwich from the bag and took a bite from it. Nerves continued to roil his stomach and he didn't want to eat. However, he also wanted to make it look as though he was here in the park for a reason, some reason other than the truth.

The sandwich became a sticky ball inside his dry mouth and he washed it down with the tea. Three children played nearby. The middle one, a slim girl with long, blond hair, threw a ball to one of the other children, who caught it and tossed it back to her. She let loose with a giggle. A smile tugged at Blair's lips, followed almost immediately by a mental image of Eleanor, face pale and still, the sound of his ex-wife sobbing, a swirl of people putting their hand on his shoulder, uncomfortably uttering words meant to comfort. The memory of his ex-wife, Daphne, sobbing, makeup smeared, cut him anew. A dull, all-too-familiar ache formed in the middle of his chest.

He set aside the sandwich. With his thumb and index finger, he reached into the breast pocket of his shirt, withdrew a phone and flipped it open. It wasn't his phone; it had shown up inside his flat—the bastards had broken into his place while he was at work—and was in a brown envelope on his kitchen table.

With his thumb, he punched in some numbers. On the third ring, a woman's voice answered.

"Yes?" the woman said.

"I got a visit," Blair said.

"Okay."

"They asked questions."

"About our friend?"

"Yes."

"And you told them what?"

"What we agreed I'd tell them. Nothing more."

"Good."

4

Malakov hung up his phone. His ever-present scowl deepened. The Russian, who'd been a bodybuilder and hockey player in his youth, remained thick in the shoulders, neck, arms and legs. He moved with a silence and grace that belied his size.

His hockey teammates had called him "Juggernaut" because, despite his size, he'd glided quickly, forcefully across the ice, and pounded his opponents. A whitish, ropelike scar ran from his temple to the bottom of his jaw, a leftover from his days as a Russian special forces soldier when he'd forced himself on a Chechen woman. She tried in vain to stop him by hitting him in the side of the head with his own vodka bottle. He still recalled how the bottle had shattered. He'd been too drunk to feel the sting of his flesh tearing open, but the haze of alcohol and time had done nothing to dim the memory of his blood bursting forth in a crimson spray on himself and the woman. A rare smile tugged at the corners of his mouth when he recalled how his blood had heightened her terror and his ardor.

Every once in a while, after he'd downed a few drinks, when talk amongst his comrades inevitably turned to sexual conquests, he'd shared that story. Occasionally, it yielded laughter, but more often than not he'd found his comrades greeted the tale with stunned silence. He chalked up their reaction to what he considered Russia's uptight sexual culture, where people repressed their primal urges. Sometimes his countrymen mystified, even disgusted him.

Hands moving on autopilot scrambled for and located a cigarette. He lit it, took a couple of drags and stared through the windows, which ran nearly from floor to ceiling, of his London penthouse. He saw from his faint reflection he was scowling again and he viewed it like the return of an old friend.

Something was wrong. John Lockwood had sounded different. Granted, he always was an uptight prick, more balls than brains, but loyal to whomever filled his bank account. Malakov had made the British prick a rich man over the last several years and had asked for nothing other than his loyalty.

Now the big Russian worried that he'd lost that. If so, that was a problem because, while he'd tried to keep as much information as possible from Lockwood, he'd had to know at least a little bit.

Enough to do whatever job Malakov had tossed his way.

If he was—how did the Americans say it?—going off the reservation... Malakov didn't finish the thought. He already knew in his gut how that play would end.

Two members of his security detachment, a couple of former Russian paratroopers, were seated at a large circular table. They smoked cigarettes, drank coffee and played cards. Malakov shook his head in disgust. Lazy bastards, born to be followers, he thought.

"Vasili," he snapped.

A compact man with neatly trimmed black hair and pale skin whipped his gaze in Malakov's direction.

"Sir?"

"You're my security chief, yes?"

Vasili looked confused. "Yes, of course."

"Yet you sit there playing cards. You think this is—what?—a retirement home? You are ready to retire, it seems."

"No, sir, of course not."

"Maybe you consider playing cards working. Maybe for someone as dim as you, that is the case."

The other man's eyes narrowed. "No, sir."

"So I am wrong," Malakov said. He allowed some menace to creep into his voice.

"Of course not," Vasili said, shaking his head no. "Perhaps I can do something for you?"

"Perhaps. John Lockwood. You do remember him, yes?"

"Of course."

"I find myself troubled. Not afraid, but troubled. I want to speak with Lockwood. Find him and bring him here."

"Of course."

"Oh, and Vasili, bring me a couple of the girls, too. I feel bored and would like some company. Perhaps tonight I can make new memories for myself."

BOLAN AND MCCARTER were seated in the Briton's new Jaguar, parked across the street from John Lockwood's strip club. Kurtzman had come up with Lockwood as a possible source of information on Yezhov since he had worked within the Russian's crime ring for years. Bolan looked at the car's steering wheel. "Nice car."

"Don't even think about it, mate," McCarter said. "I don't even like you being in the same country as one of my cars. You'll drive it over my dead body."

"Only if there were no other escape routes."

"Funny," McCarter said, swigging from his can of Coke. "Laugh riot is what you are."

McCarter stared through the windshield. Bolan followed his gaze and saw a trio of women. All were dressed in low-cut blouses, short skirts and stiletto heels, huddled together near the mouth of an alley, talking.

"Normally, I hate stakeouts," McCarter said, grinning. "Don't like to sit still this long. But considering the view, I am willing to make the sacrifice."

Bolan nodded, but said nothing. No doubt, the women who'd stopped by the car were attractive. They'd dutifully flirted and joked with the two men until it became apparent they were not going to make a sale. Then they'd moved on.

"You two are either cops or fags," a young redhead had snapped.

"Wrong on both counts," McCarter had called after her.

Finally, thirty minutes later, the women had stopped coming by.

McCarter again turned to Bolan. "You know, it's going to look suspicious, us just sitting out here. Being a John isn't a spectator sport, last I checked. We're going to get pegged as cops."

"You thinking of sampling the merchandise?"

"Anything for the cause," McCarter said. "No, I'm just thinking we may want to move on, if nothing happens. Maybe find another spot to watch the goings on."

Bolan nodded. "You're probably right."

McCarter grabbed the ignition key. But before he could turn it, a black SUV cruised by, streetlights gleaming white on the vehicle's tinted windows. The SUV slowed at the mouth of an alley next to Lockwood's strip club, turned. Bolan glanced at McCarter, who was also watching the vehicle. Then he popped open his door and went EVA.

He darted across the street. Tires squealed against the pavement as drivers braked hard to avoid hitting the warrior. Irritated drivers honked their horns or flashed their bright headlights at Bolan. The soldier tuned them out and focused his attention on the alley.

Once he'd made it to the sidewalk, he noticed the tail end of McCarter's Jaguar as the vehicle sped to the nearest corner, slowed and turned. He unzipped his coat, reached inside and drew the Beretta from its shoulder holster, but kept the gun hidden beneath the jacket.

Bolan walked along the front of Lockwood's club. When he reached the alley, he stopped and peered around the corner. The black SUV stood in the alley. The vehicle's engine idled, belching a whitish exhaust from the tailpipe.

Two shadows disembarked from the vehicle and walked toward the club. One of them opened the club's side door and both figures disappeared through it.

Bolan keyed his throat microphone.

"Two just went inside," he said. "Unsure if we have any more in the vehicle."

"Roger that," McCarter replied.

Bolan heard a door latch click and he froze. The soldier melted into the shadows and pressed his body against the club.

The rear passenger's-side door flipped open and a man stepped from the vehicle. The guy was tall and lanky. His bald pate gleamed under the glow from the single exposed bulb moored to the club. An unlit cigarette dangled from his lips. He slammed his door. A second man stepped from the driver's seat, a pump shotgun held in his hands. He rounded the rear of the SUV and moved toward the other guy.

"Hope Lockwood's here," said the guy with the shotgun. Bolan noticed the man spoke English with a thick accent. "Malakov's going to have our asses if we don't bring this guy back with us."

"Don't worry," the bald guy replied. "Lockwood's here. He's not the type to run."

"Gutsy?"

Mr. Shotgun laughed and shook his head. "Try greedy. He's got his club. He's got a couple of flats in London and some collectible cars. He won't leave all that behind. He'd try to swim with gold bricks in his pocket, if he could."

Bolan ran the numbers. He figured the two guys inside likely would make it to Lockwood's office in less than a minute.

The soldier stepped from the shadows. The man holding the shotgun apparently caught the movement from the corner of his eye, wheeled toward Bolan's direction and raised the weapon to his shoulder in one fluid movement. But Bolan had the drop on the guy and triggered the Beretta. The handgun chugged out a tri-burst, the bullets ripping into the guy's torso. The impact caused him to backpedal a couple of steps before he crumpled to the ground in a boneless heap.

The second guy, eyes wide with surprise, clawed underneath his jacket for hardware. The Beretta coughed out another burst and the slugs drilled into the thug's chest. Even as the guy folded to the ground, Bolan stalked past him to the club's side door.

The Executioner opened the door and saw it led into a storage room at the rear of the club. The Beretta poised before him, he stepped inside, closed the door. Steel shelves stood one behind the next, loaded with boxes of liquor and snacks. He strained his ears for signs of the two other gunners. The only sound he heard was heavy metal music, muffled but discernible, as it ground out of the club's sound system. Exiting the storeroom, he stepped into a brightly lit corridor, the same one he'd been through earlier that led to Lockwood's office.

The Executioner glided down the corridor, past the doors of what he assumed were rooms for private shows. When he got within a dozen steps or so of Lockwood's office, he heard Lockwood's voice, taut and loud, emanating through the closed door.

"The bloke had a gun on me, what was I supposed to do?"

"Quiet!"

His fingers wrapped around the knob, the soldier gave it a gentle twist. It moved a quarter inch or so, stopped. It was locked.

The big American stepped back, aimed the Beretta's muzzle on the lock, fired. The bullet pierced the steel, destroying the lock. Bolan raised his foot, slammed it against the door. It swung inward, the soldier following behind it.

Even as he barreled through the door, Bolan sized up the situation. Lockwood remained, where Bolan had left him earlier, trussed up to the chair. His bodyguard still lay on the floor, sleeping off the beating he'd received less than an hour ago from McCarter. One of the Russians stood before Lockwood, left fist cocked on his hip, right hand clutching a Glock with a sound suppressor screwed into the barrel. The other stood forty-five degrees to Bolan's right. His back was to Lockwood, while he stared at a small bank of television monitors that Bolan had noticed earlier. Cameras feeding the monitors peeked into the private rooms. An MP-5 submachine gun filled his right hand. The barrel, also fixed with a sound suppressor, was pointed toward the floor. But the commotion finally yanked his attention from the skin show unfolding on the monitors. His gaze was whipping in Bolan's direction and he was flicking the cigarette away as the MP-5 swung up.

The Beretta sighed once and a hole opened in the Russian's forehead. The Executioner watched as the man's body went slack. Even as the shooter collapsed to the ground, a bullet sizzled past Bolan's neck. The soldier whirled toward the second Russian, the Beretta tracking in on the man. The handgun coughed once and a 9 mm slug lanced into the guy's shoulder. A cry erupted from his lips and the Glock tumbled to the ground.

To his credit, the man recovered quickly from the pain of the gunshot, he bent down to get the pistol.

But with a couple of long strides, Bolan closed the distance between them and drove a foot into the man's chest. The Russian shooter fell onto his behind with a grunt. The Executioner set his booted foot onto the man's lost weapon and centered the Beretta's muzzle on the man's forehead.

"Stop," Bolan said.

Instinctively, the man tried to raise his hands. He winced, grunted and stuck his good hand in the air. The guy glanced at the injury. Bolan looked at it, too, saw a dark shiny stain had formed around the bullet's entry point. The man shifted his gaze to Bolan.

"I'm bleeding," he said.

"And I bleed for you," Bolan said.

McCarter's voice buzzed in Bolan's earpiece. In the same instant, both Lockwood and the Russian began peppering Bolan with expletive-filled tirades. The soldier tuned them out and keyed his microphone.

"Go," Bolan said.

"Outside's still clear," McCarter said. "Need me to come in?"

Bolan did and told him so.

Signing off, Bolan turned to the Russian. The guy's skin had paled from the blood loss and Bolan guessed the man would go into shock soon. He had to move quickly.

"How are you feeling?" Bolan asked.

"I told you I am bleeding, you fuck," the guy replied. "I'm going to bleed to death."

Bolan shook his head. "Doubt it," he said. "Not from that wound. Oh, you'll bleed. But it would take a while before you actually bleed out."

Bolan paused a couple of beats. Then he waved the Beretta. "This is a Beretta 93-R. Shoots 9 millimeter rounds. Whisper-quiet, which is nice. I like that. But what I really like is that it fires three bullets at a time. Very handy."

The man's gaze was intent on Bolan, but he didn't seem to be following what the soldier was saying.

"Now the gutshot?" he said. "The one I am about to give you? That's going to really screw you up. Three bullets can tear the hell out of your organs. Maybe pierce your spine. I'm not a doctor, but you get a wound like that—" Bolan shrugged "—bleeding is the least of your worries."

Another pause.

"Upside is, you won't have to worry long. You'll welcome death."

Bolan saw the light go on in the guy's eyes. The Russian licked his lips.

"What do you want?" the man said.

"Information."

"Fine."

THE HINTON TOWER stood among the office towers in London's financial district. It's hide of mirrored windows caught the spectrum of lights emanating from traffic signals and streetlights, and corporate signs moored to neighboring office towers.

The Executioner stepped from the shadows of an alley that ran between the Hinton Tower and its closest neighbor, a skyscraper that housed a global bank. A black nylon briefcase hung from his right shoulder. McCarter emerged a heartbeat later, a nearly identical briefcase slung over his shoulder.

Bolan's ice-blue eyes surveyed the building's exterior, matched it with the intelligence he'd gained. The thug who had given them this intel worked for a man named Malakov—who just so happened to be a high-ranking associate of Mikhail Yezhov. Malakov, once a tenant in the building, had bought it out of receivership after the bottom fell out of London's commercial real estate market. That transaction had allowed him to install a tighter security. This included plainclothes, armed guards in the lobby, tougher firewalls on the computers managing the security system and a rooftop helipad to allow for private departures.

"Nice digs," McCarter muttered.

Bolan nodded.

"You think our boy's information was good?"

"He was about to bleed out," Bolan replied. "What do you think?"

"Impending death makes for a hell of a truth serum. Good job bandaging him up, by the way."

"Thanks."

"Seems a little counterproductive, this whole shooting-people-then-tending-to-their-wounds thing," McCarter said.

Bolan shrugged. "Made a deal with the guy. Not sure he deserved to live, but I made a deal. I don't think he's going to bother anybody for a while. MI5 was going to send in a cleanup team, take him to a hospital. They'll extradite him."

"So we can shoot him again, at another time in another place."

"Gives us something to look forward to," Bolan said.

"True that."

By this point, the soldier and McCarter had reached the line of glass doors leading into the tower's lobby. Despite the hour, the revolving door spun easily, spitting Bolan, then McCarter, into the lobby. A handful of men and women, well-groomed professional people in suits, strode purposefully in a dozen different directions through the lobby. This didn't surprise Bolan. The Russian had told him that Malakov ran a massive energy-and-stock futures operation on the building's first two floors. With the staff making trades globally, people populated the building around the clock.

A pair of burly men togged in navy blue sport coats, gray slacks and red ties were seated behind an information desk that stood in the middle of the lobby. The Stony Man warriors approached the desk. The guards, who'd been talking, fell silent and looked at Bolan and McCarter.

"Help you?" the younger man asked.

"Have some documents to drop off," McCarter said. He patted his briefcase to emphasize the point.

"Documents for who?"

"Apex Trading," McCarter said. "On the twenty-second floor."

"I know what floor it's on," the man said. "Who at Apex?"

"Ed Haggar." Kurtzman had grabbed the names with an internet search and fed them to Bolan.

The young man shook his head. "Don't know him."

"Your loss." McCarter nodded at a phone. "Want to call him and verify?"

The guard seemed to contemplate this for a couple of seconds, then shook his head.

"Nah," he said. "Sign in, go on up."

The guard handed them a clipboard with a sign-up sheet on it. They dutifully signed fake personal and employer names. Handing the clipboard back to the guard, they headed for the elevators.

"So much for the tighter security. Thanks for doing the talking," Bolan said as they walked away.

"My British accent versus your Yank accent gives them one less red flag."

"I could've faked it."

"And sounded like a constipated butler from central bloody casting? No, thanks."

"Let's step it up," Bolan said. "They're going to figure out their people aren't coming back soon. Things'll heat up then."

They rode the elevator to the twenty-second floor, exited and climbed the stairs another seven stories, in case the guards bothered to monitor the elevator traffic. The twenty-ninth floor contained Malokov's personal offices, while his penthouse was located on the floor above that. They stepped into the reception area, which was fully carpeted and paneled with caramel-colored wood. While fully lit, the area stood empty and silent.

The Russian at the strip club had given Bolan a brief description of the building's top two floors. The cyberwarriors at Stony Man Farm had done their best to confirm as many details as possible. Bolan surveyed his surroundings and saw behind a receptionist's desk stood a double door. From what the Executioner knew, the doors led into the inner offices of Malakov's operations. A private elevator to the Russian mobster's penthouse was also beyond the door.

The soldier nudged McCarter with an elbow and nodded in return toward the door. McCarter nodded. Bolan unzipped the nylon case he carried, dipped a hand inside and felt around for the pistol grip of the Heckler & Koch MP-5 submachine gun. Sliding the weapon out, he next pulled a sound suppressor from the bag, and threaded it into the SMG's barrel. McCarter had pulled a similar weapon from his own briefcase and was also outfitting it with a sound suppressor.

The big American slipped the MP-5's safety off. Silent as a wraith, he glided across the office to the door. From beyond the door, he heard the murmur of voices. A quick glance over his shoulder at McCarter elicited a nod from the Briton, indicating that he heard the voices, too.

The soldier carefully gripped the doorknob and gave it a gentle twist. It turned easily. He pushed the door inward, saw a long corridor lay ahead. Doors branched off from either side, presumably leading into offices. The MP-5 poised at shoulder level, the soldier pressed ahead. The first couple of doors he passed were closed, the interior lights extinguished, but the voices continued to grow louder.

As he took several long strides, the voices—both male—became louder. They spoke in a language Bolan recognized as Russian, though he only understood a phrase or two from their conversation. A door stood open a few paces ahead and to his right. Cigarette smoke wafted from the room and into the hallway.

Bolan peered around the door frame. Inside the room, a trim middle-aged man stared out the window, puffing on a cigarette. Bolan noted the pistol holstered in the small his back. The man's fists were cocked on his hips and he was speaking.

A second man sat on the edge of a desk, one leg extended until his foot touched the floor, the other foot dangling well off the floor, swinging like a pendulum. A salt-and-pepper beard, trimmed close, covered the lower half of his face. He held his pump shotgun by its pistol grip, the tip of his index finger tapping against the outer front curve of the trigger guard. The slide rested on the top of his right thigh.

The man who'd been staring out the window suddenly fell silent. Bolan realized the guy had caught sight of Bolan's reflection in the window.

Cigarette still clenched in his jaw, the thug wheeled around, his hand clawing for the holstered pistol. Bolan's MP-5 chugged out a quick burst. The bullets punched into the guy's chest and shoved him against the window. Even as the corpse collapsed to the floor in a boneless heap, the bearded man with the shotgun responded with the reflexes of a pro, his weapon in motion, muzzle hunting a target.

Bolan whipped toward the second shooter. Before the warrior could line up a shot, the other man's weapon thundered. The hastily placed round flew wide of Bolan, ripping through the door frame and Sheetrock to the Executioner's left. Splintered wood bit into Bolan's cheek and his left hand—the hand holding the weapon's front stock. A fast burst lashed from the MP-5's muzzle. The 9 mm manglers buzzed just past the shooter's ear. He thrust himself from the desktop, fired once more while in motion. In the same instant, Bolan spun away from the doorway, and the shotgun blast tore through the space where he had just stood.

From inside the room, Bolan heard the metallic snick of a shotgun slide being worked as his enemy chambered another round. The soldier, still in a crouch, rounded the door frame. In the same instant, he spotted the shotgun's muzzle swinging back in his direction as the thug drew down on the door. Bolan squeezed the MP-5's trigger, letting loose with a burst of parabellum rounds that slammed into the man's rib cage, and spun him a quarter turn. Shock etched on his face, the shooter staggered back a couple of steps before he collapsed to the ground.

Moving in a crouch, Bolan stepped farther into the room, searching it for other threats. The close-quarters shotgun blast still rang in his ears, but beyond that, Bolan heard a strained voice emanating from an as-yet-unseen radio handset. The soldier moved to the closest fallen guard, kicked the shotgun away and knelt next to the man. Hands sifted through the dead man's pockets, but came up empty. The soldier noticed a thin gold chain looped around the man's neck. With a curled index finger, he lifted the chain, saw a key and a card with a magnetic strip hanging from it. Curling his fingers around the chain, he yanked it hard and it broke. Discarding the broken chain, he pocketed the key and the card. The soldier gathered up the dead man's radio. He moved to the other corpse and shoved the man's keys, card and radio into the pockets of his leather jacket.

Coming to his feet, he strode from the room. McCarter stood in the hallway, the MP-5 at the ready as he stood watch.

"Anything?" the Briton asked.

With a nod, Bolan handed McCarter a key, a card and a radio. The former SAS commando stuffed the key and the card into the pocket of his khaki pants, and held on to the radio.

"Keys or the card probably operate the penthouse elevator," Bolan said.

At this point, Bolan detected an edge of panic in the voice coming from the radio.

"You realize they've heard us."

"Probably," Bolan said. "Considering Malakov's line of work, I'm guessing there's soundproofing between the floors. Enough to muffle a shotgun blast? Maybe not. Regardless, they've lost contact with two men. They're going to react."

The radios went silent.

A grim smile played over McCarter's lips. "That's a good sign."

OVER THE YEARS, Malakov had bragged more than once that his living room could hold his childhood apartment five times over. The room, with its vaulted ceilings and contemporary furniture, hummed with activity as he entered. He watched with grim satisfaction as security guards jogged in different directions through the room, taking up positions behind overturned tables, guns trained on the elevator. The security chief waded into the bustle. With the practiced smoothness of an orchestra conductor, he used hand signals to move individual gunners into their position. The man had been one of Russia's best special forces commanders before Malakov had recruited him to lead his private security detail. The man had taken an already decent cadre of security guards and whipped them into top shape.

Malakov swept his gaze over the room again. He counted at least a dozen men, most armed with submachine guns while a few clutched Glocks or other handguns. Some had donned Kevlar vests and ballistic helmets.

He spun on a heel, strode to his office. A grim smile played over his lips.

Nothing would get through that, he told himself. Nothing.

5

Bolan was crouched to one side of the elevator door. His heart rate and breathing accelerated with each passing moment. Blood thundered in his ears. The soldier willed his breathing to slow, his thoughts to remain rational, despite the bucket loads of adrenaline being pumped into his system.

He glanced across the car, saw McCarter pressed against the wall beneath the control panel, body coiled tightly.

The car slid to a stop. Bolan tensed.

As the doors hissed open, he keyed the microphone.

"Now," he whispered.

The doors parted halfway before the first shots lanced into the elevator car. The familiar rattle of submachine guns, accompanied by the occasional crack of a handgun, sounded from outside the elevator. A hail of bullets swarmed into the confined space. Slugs tore into the walls at the rear of the elevator car, shredding the interior. Bolan ground his teeth, waited.

Suddenly, the relentless pounding from a helicopter's chain gun pealed in the night. Glass shattered and swarms of bullets ripped through flesh. From the first rattle of the chain gun, Bolan counted to ten.

The withering fire stopped almost as quickly as it had begun. Bolan tossed the flash-bang grenade through the door. The orb struck the floor with a clatter. One of the already panicked shooters let loose with a terrified scream. Within a couple of heartbeats, the weapon exploded with a flash of white light and a loud bang.

Bolan uncoiled from the floor. From the edge of his vision, he could tell McCarter was also in motion. The Executioner moved in a crouch through the elevator door, the MP-5 hunting a target, while his ice-blue eyes took in the mayhem that lay before them. Unrelenting gunfire had disintegrated windows. The muted sounds of nighttime traffic filtered through the openings. Glass shards littered the floor and the furniture. Bullet holes pierced a bar that stood along one wall. The fabric of couches and chairs had been ripped apart.

Dead shooters lay on the floor, torsos and limbs rent by the merciless assault. Other bodies were draped over furniture. Motion caught Bolan's eye. He swerved his head to the left, saw two gunners, bodies bloodied. One man was curled in a fetal position, groaning. A second lay on his back, his body convulsing as life slipped away. With bursts from the MP-5, Bolan ended each man's suffering, dispatching them to hell. McCarter's own weapon fired and he took out two more wounded men.

Bolan rolled through the room, left the slaughter in his rearview mirror and moved into a corridor that led off the main room. He found another shooter, one thigh chewed up by autofire, sprawled on floor, a pool of blood widening beneath him. Judging by the crimson smear staining the hardwood floor, Bolan guessed the man probably had dragged himself from the shooting gallery in the main room, seeking refuge here. The body was still. Bolan knelt next to the fallen man, rolled him over. Sightless eyes stared up at the warrior. Bolan checked for a pulse, found none. A bullet must have hit an artery and caused the man to bleed out, Bolan thought.

McCarter already had moved past the soldier and was checking the rooms that led from the hallway. Bolan stood up and began doing the same, clearing two.

Bolan quickly felt impatience welling up inside him. They'd made a hell of a noise getting here, and the soldier wanted to grab Malakov and get the hell out of here quickly. The last thing he needed was a confrontation with the British authorities. That meant not waiting around for them. He figured Brognola could smooth it over, eventually, but the soldier couldn't afford to have his wings clipped even for a short time.

By this point Bolan had switched the MP-5 to a one-handed grip and removed a second flash-bang grenade from inside his jacket. One room remained unchecked. Bolan and McCarter took up positions on either side of it. The Executioner nodded at McCarter, then toward the door, and held up the flash-bang. The Briton nodded his understanding, ready for what came next.

SWEAT BEADED ON Malakov's scalp and streamed in rivulets down his face. It slicked his palms, which were wrapped around the Uzi's pistol grip. Fear cinched steel bands around his chest, drew them tight and forced his breath to come in shallow pulls.

He wasn't afraid, he assured himself. He'd been in at least a dozen firefights in Chechnya and later when he ran black ops inside the state of Georgia during its brief conflict with Russia.

It's just the surprise, he told himself. The adrenaline that surged through him.

He'd heard the brief explosion of gunfire. Even muted by the walls, his trained ear still could tell it was a large-caliber machine gun. The thrum of chopper blades only confirmed it.

Who the hell were these people? They weren't locals, he thought with certainty. They'd not handle a raid like this—hitting him with two armed men and a helicopter. They'd stream in, togged in police uniforms and armed with search warrants. Besides, he'd greased enough palms that, were something like this coming down, he'd have known about it ahead of time. The CIA? It was possible, he supposed. He'd been shipping weapons to the Taliban, both in Pakistan and Afghanistan. Same went for al Qaeda. But he'd encountered Agency spooks before. They might try something like this in Mogadishu, but not in the middle of London.

Before he could follow the train of thought any further, a loud thump at the door snagged his attention, caused his stomach to plummet. He wheeled toward the door, saw the wood around the knob splinter. The door whipped open.

He raised his weapon, curled his finger around the trigger.

MCCARTER SPUN AWAY from the kicked-open door, flattening himself against a wall just outside it.

A blast of submachine-gun fire lanced through the doorway. Bolan judged it would have struck McCarter in the chest had he not moved. The Executioner was coiled low to the floor, against the wall next to the door, his arm lashed out and around its frame. Fingers uncurled and released the grenade.

The gun fell silent. An instant later, a loud pop sounded from within the room. A white flash flared through the doorway, momentarily overtaking the other lights before it receded.

The soldier peered around the door frame. Inside the room, he saw Malakov, his Uzi still in his grip, but aimed at nothing. His free hand was cupped over his corresponding ear. He looked dazed. Bolan surged into the room, crossing it in quick strides. McCarter was a couple of steps behind.

"Drop it!" Bolan ordered.

Malakov, still dazed, looked in the soldier's direction. Bolan tensed, wondering for a moment whether the guy would make a fatal play. The Russian unclenched his fist. The Uzi dropped to the floor with a clatter and he raised his hands.

BOLAN GAVE MALAKOV a hard shove between the shoulder blades. The force hurtled him through the door and onto the rooftop. Jack Grimaldi's chopper stood on the helipad, the blades whirring.

Once he caught his footing, Malakov, his hands bound behind him by plastic handcuffs, turned around toward the Stony Man warriors.

"Who the hell are you?" he demanded. He had to shout to be heard above the growl of the helicopter's engines and the thrum of the spinning blades. "Where are you taking me?"

Bolan closed the distance between them, grabbed Malakov by the biceps and spun him around. He jabbed the muzzle of his MP-5 into the guy's ribs to end the conversation, and then marched him to the helicopter.

The soldier saw the helicopter's side door stood open. Chad Ramirez, one of the Stony Man blacksuits, stood in the doorway. A skilled pilot and a former U.S. Air Force special ops soldier,

Ramirez had been Grimaldi's copilot for the long trip from Virginia to London. With quick, efficient moves, Ramirez grabbed Malakov, shoved him into a seat and fitted a safety harness on him. McCarter shut the door. Bolan dropped into the seat next to Malakov and strapped himself in.

Grimaldi took the bird into the air and flew it from the city's center. A short while later, he put the helicopter down at a small airport on the outskirts of London. The Executioner, McCarter, Grimaldi and the Russian disembarked from the aircraft. As soon as they'd put several yards between them and the helicopter, Ramirez took the craft up into the air, spun it forty-five degrees, gunned the engine and flew into the darkness.

Bolan knew Ramirez was supposed to take the craft to a potato farm owned by a CIA asset, who'd agreed, for a price, to store it in one of his barns. A car would be waiting to whisk Ramirez away.

A pair of black SUVs stood on the tarmac. McCarter broke away from the group, double-timed it to one of the vehicles and climbed into the driver's seat. The rear hatch popped open.

Malakov looked at the cramped space, then at Bolan.

"You're not putting me in there!" he protested.

Bolan's right fist lashed out and struck the Russian in the temple. The guy's eyes rolled back in his head, his knees buckled and he sank to the ground.

Bolan and Grimaldi hefted the guy and stuffed him into the space. Bolan grabbed the edge of a navy blue blanket that dangled over the back of the nearest seat. Yanking it down, he covered Malakov and shut the hatch. Bolan watched Grimaldi climb into the front passenger seat and shut the door. McCarter gunned the engine. The SUV lurched forward and was rolling across the tarmac even as Bolan made his way to the second vehicle. By the time he'd climbed into the driver's seat, the crimson glow from the taillights of McCarter's SUV were shrinking in the distance.

THE SAFE HOUSE WAS a vacant apartment located on London's east side, on the second floor above a small computer repair shop.

Malakov sat on a couch, feet flat on the floor, hands cuffed behind his back. An electric fan whirred in the background. Bolan had turned on the television to add more background noise. Small devices built into each window emitted high-pitched sound waves that caused the glass to vibrate, an old trick aimed at foiling eavesdroppers.

The soldier stood in front of Malakov. Five feet or so separated the two men. Bolan, hands hanging loose at his sides, stared down at the Russian, who returned Bolan's cold stare with one of his own.

McCarter sat at an oval-shaped dining table, the top scarred with deep gouges in the caramel-colored wood. He'd lined up four magazines, each on its side, on the tabletop. He clutched a fifth magazine in his left hand and with his right loaded the first of thirteen rounds into it. Grimaldi stood in the kitchen, lanky frame leaning against the sink, and puffed on a cigarette.

Malakov all but ignored the other two men and focused on Bolan, apparently convinced that the big American was running the show.

"For why do you bring me here?" the Russian demanded, his accent thick.

McCarter, without looking up from his work, snorted. "To admire your command of English."

"What?" Malakov asked, his voice a snarl.

"He means cut the crap," Bolan interjected. "Your father was the Soviet Union's ambassador to London. You lived here more than you did Moscow growing up. Even went to Oxford. Save the language-barrier act for someone who believes it."

Malakov didn't blink.

"That was before the GRU shipped you off to Chechnya, right?" Bolan said.

"You have me at a disadvantage," Malakov said.

"Understatement," Grimaldi said.

The Russian whipped his head toward the pilot, the skin of his neck turning a deep scarlet.

"What did you say?" he demanded.

Grimaldi yawned and swigged coffee from a mug.

Malakov turned his gaze back in Bolan's direction. "You'll regret this."

Bolan pivoted on his heel, walked to the table where McCarter sat. He grabbed one of the chairs, carried it back to the spot where he'd stood a few moments ago and set it on the floor, its back facing Malakov. The soldier dropped into the seat, a thigh jutting from either side of the chair's back, forearms resting on the top rail of the chair's back. He shed his jacket and draped it over an arm of the couch.

"Why is Yezhov so hell bent on getting the Nightingale?" he asked.

"He doesn't tell me such things."

"Too bad for you."

Malakov licked his lips.

"He doesn't tell me such things," he repeated. This time, though, Bolan thought he detected an edge in the other man's voice.

"He still looking for her?"

"I don't—"

"Like I said, cut the crap," Bolan said, emphasizing each word.

A rivulet of sweat trickled down from Malakov's temple.

"He still looking for her?"

"Yes."

"Getting his own hands dirty?"

"What?" Malakov paused. "Is he doing it himself? No, he has people do it for him."

"The looking?"

"The looking."

"And the killing."

"I don't know—" Malakov apparently caught himself and paused. "He has other worries."

"He's the big-picture guy."

"He has other priorities."

"Such as?"

"Those are—what's the expression?—above my pay grade."

"Somehow I doubt that."

The soldier felt his own impatience rising, tinged with uncertainty. Either Malakov was really as out of the loop as he professed or he was jerking Bolan around. The latter scenario struck Bolan as the most likely one. Regardless, things were not going to end well for Malakov.

The Executioner heaved a sigh, stood up and drew a bead on the Russian's forehead with the Beretta.

"Sorry," Bolan said, his voice sounding anything but. "I've had my crap quota for the day."

Bolan saw something flicker in Malakov's eyes before it was gone again.

"You would kill me?"

"Yes."

"I told you what I know."

"Massive data dump," Bolan said. "Thanks."

Malakov shifted slightly in his seat. Bolan could all but hear the wheels turning in the guy's head.

"Perhaps it's how you ask the questions," Malakov said. "It has been a long, difficult night."

"Here's my counter," Bolan said. "Stop jerking me around. Answer my questions, fast. In case you haven't noticed, there's no bargaining table between us."

Bolan waited several seconds in silence, letting Malakov consider his words. He heard the scratch of a lighter being struck and a heartbeat later caught the first whiff of Grimaldi's cigarette. In the same moment, he heard McCarter feed a magazine into what he assumed was the Browning, heard the Phoenix Force commando working the slide, chambering a round.

"Why does Yezhov want Nightingale?"

"She stole his money. Lots of it."

"So he ordered a hit?"

"Yes."

"Of his own accord."

"Of course, yes."

"He has the juice to do that all by himself?"

"Of course."

"Why draw all the attention?"

Malakov gave a slight shrug. "He miscalculated."

"Meaning?"

"He thought she'd be an easy mark. He was wrong. He hired two amateurs, in my opinion. They screwed it up. I told him not to hire them."

"Because?"

"They're stupid, sloppy. If he'd hired someone more trustworthy, with better tradecraft, you and I wouldn't be talking right now."

"Because she'd be dead?"

"Because she'd be dead, yes. She'd also be all but useless, a sack of skin and bones."

"That doesn't mean we wouldn't be hunting you."

Malakov gave a derisive snort and shook his head pityingly.

"You don't believe that any more than I do. The woman's value is all the things floating around in her head. The account numbers, the names, the other intelligence she has gathered over the years. I have no idea who you're with. CIA? NSA? SEAL Team Six? Definitely not FBI, with the way you throw bullets around. Doesn't matter. You want what's in her head. You don't give a fuck about her any more than I do or Yezhov does."

Bolan guessed the guy was playing him and decided to change the subject.

"Fair enough," the Executioner said. "And what does she know that Yezhov wants?"

"I told you, he wants his money back. That's all."

"How did he find her in the first place?" Bolan asked. "She's been on the run for years."

"Yezhov has sources. Don't bother asking me who—I don't know. I just know he was able to turn someone in her network. Her location was a last-minute tip. I thought it was bullshit. Frankly, I guessed it was a setup of some kind. Malakov had been beating the bushes for her for months. I thought someone had decided to flag us on and it would turn out to be a lie."

"For what reason?"

Malakov shrugged. "The possibilities are endless. Maybe a competitor hoped to distract him or to humiliate him. Drive him crazy, perhaps. It's hard to say. In the end, I was wrong and he was right. She was exactly where his source said she'd be."

"Yet you lost her."

Malakov's eyes narrowed. He drew in a big breath of air, swelled his chest out, exhaled slowly.

"I lost no one. I never wanted to hire those two men. I would have handled it much differently."

"Spare me the strategy lecture," Bolan said.

Malakov shrugged.

Bolan opened his mouth to speak, but checked himself. A nearby table lamp began flashing, stopping Bolan in midsentence.

Bolan looked at McCarter, who was already on his feet.

The soldier drew his Beretta and started for the door.

Something thudded against it and it swung inward.

A man dressed in a black leather bomber jacket, his face covered with a black ski mask, stood in the doorway. He swung a sound-suppressed Glock in Bolan's direction. The Executioner dived to the floor just as the weapon coughed twice. Still laying on his side, he raised the Beretta. Before he could squeeze off a shot, gunfire crackled from Bolan's left and bullets ripped into the man, causing him to jerk in place.

A glance over his shoulder and he saw McCarter, smoke still curling from the barrel of his weapon, moving for Malakov.

A second shooter, this one also masked, came through the door. He aimed his pistol at Malakov and fired twice. Bolan aimed his own weapon at the guy and fired. A pair of tri-bursts drilled into the man's torso and he crumpled to the ground.

Bolan whirled toward Malakov. The man was heaped on the floor, blood flowing from a wound in his temple.

McCarter, who'd been kneeling next to the Russian, looked at Bolan and shook his head.

"Dead," he said.

The Stony Man warriors searched the building. Bolan found the man who ran the electronics shop slumped over a counter, dead from a bullet wound to the back of his head. If Yezhov had sent anyone else, they'd fled.

When they returned to the second floor, the soldier phoned

Stony Man Farm and asked for them to send a cleanup crew. The upper floor had been soundproofed, so that had at least prevented anyone from hearing the gunfire from McCarter's weapon.

"How'd they find us?" McCarter asked.

Bolan shrugged. "Maybe they followed us. Maybe Malakov had a microchip sewn into his clothes. Hard to know."

McCarter nodded. "What's our next move?"

"Look for another stone to turn over," Bolan replied.

6

Nigel Lawson shut the locker door, leaned forward and rested his forehead against it. The steel felt cool and comforting against his skin. He squeezed his eyes shut and wished in vain that his reality belonged to someone else. How could he do this to her? The thought raced over and over in his head, like a pop-song chorus that had wormed its way into his subconscious and refused to let go.

Pulling his head away from the locker, he opened his eyes and slipped the key into the pocket of his frayed jeans.

He walked a few steps, halted. Commuters pushed past him, obviously unaware of the conflict raging inside the shabby man.

Though normally he was tuned in to his surroundings when he made a drop, the passersby on this day seemed little more than a noisy blur. He drew his hand from his pocket, uncurled his thick fingers and studied the locker key that rested in his sweat-slicked palm. A cloak of guilt hung from his shoulders and felt heavy enough to push his legs through concrete and into the earth like two fence posts. The thought continued: how could he do this to her? He was one of the few people she trusted and he'd just helped destroy her.

He shoved the key back into his jeans pocket and started moving again. The underground station suddenly felt hot and confining. He headed for the nearest stairwell and inserted himself into the crush of people heading upstairs.

His mind returned to the key, then to the package he'd left in the locker. You have no choice, he reminded himself. The Russians have you by the balls. Pretending otherwise is a fool's play.

He remembered the package that the craggy-faced Russian, Mikoyan, had brought him.

Lawson had taken the package, slammed the door in Mikoyan's face and ripped off the plain brown wrapping paper, opened the box and reached in. He had found twenty folders inside. He'd picked up the first folder, fanned it open, studied the black-and-white photograph stapled inside. An icy fist of fear immediately had buried itself in his gut. It was his mother and father. They were seated at an outdoor café that he didn't recognize. Once Jimmy had died, they'd relocated to California. Too many bad memories in London, they'd said. They wanted a fresh start. Neither was looking directly at the camera, but he recognized them easily. He dropped into a chair and examined the contents of the other folders. Each contained pictures of relatives, both in the United Kingdom and over in the United States.

Also in the box was a mobile phone. When it rang, he nearly jumped out of his skin. The caller had identified himself as Yezhov and laid out a proposal.

"One life or twenty," Yezhov had told him. "You thought losing one man, your brother, was hard. That it changed your life? Left you bitter? Imagine twenty. Maybe more. And this time every drop of blood would be on your hands. Think about that."

Lawson recalled how his grip on the phone had tightened. A mixture of terror and anger roiling his insides as the other man's words sank in.

"You wouldn't do that," Lawson had said.

"We both know I would."

Lawson wasn't sure what had chilled him more, the man's calm, almost bored tone as he discussed killing twenty people, or the certainty of his threat.

Finally, his shoulders had sagged in surrender. Yezhov was right. Lawson knew if he didn't adhere to the man's demands, people, lots of people, would die.

"You son of a bitch," Lawson had muttered.

"I'll send you a package. You make sure it gets into the woman's hands. Do that and you can walk away, hands clean."

Lawson made a noise, signifying his disgust. Neither his hands nor his conscience would be clean when all this was over.

"You plan to kill her."

"Not necessarily," Yezhov had answered. "I need to speak to her. She'd never come if I made the call, would she? She'd run like hell. A word of advice? Don't think about what's going to happen to her. Just do your small part and go back to your little life."

Nigel, speaking through clenched teeth, had said, "Fine."

"Good, open your front door. You'll find another box sitting in front of it. The man who'd dropped off the last package—his name's Mikoyan—left it. The box contains a telephone. You deliver new phones to the Nightingale when she's in your country, yes?"

"Yes."

"Take this to whatever prearranged spot you have. Leave it along with any other items you had planned to give her. Do that and we'll leave you alone."

"How do you know all this stuff? How we operate?"

"I won't answer that. Oh, and one other thing."

"Jesus—what?"

"I need you to make another phone call. This one to the United States. I'll even tell you what to say."

"Who am I calling this time?"

Yezhov recited a number and Lawson felt his knees turn rubbery.

"Look—"

"Don't screw this up, Nigel," Yezhov had warned. "We're tracking your phone calls. Going through your emails. As the Americans would say, you're my little bitch now. If you feel the urge to improvise, squelch it. Otherwise, think of the gallons of blood I'll spill in your name. Now, go. You have a phone call to make."

The line went dead. The Briton turned off his own phone, heaved it across the room. An enraged scream welled up inside him, burst from his lips. Dropping into a nearby chair, he covered his face with his hands, shook his head from side to side, his brain refusing to accept just how out of control his life had suddenly become.

The bastard was absolutely right. Lawson set aside the mobile phone Yezhov had sent him and made the other call.

God help him, he'd dialed the number and said the words that Yezhov had scripted for him almost verbatim. As soon as he'd hung up the phone, he'd wanted to pick it back up, call his friend and shout a warning. Instead, he'd opened his apartment door and found the promised package sitting in the hallway. Swallowing hard, he'd carried it into the apartment.

And here he was doing the Devil's work. One life or twenty. The words chilled him. He really had no choice, did he?

LAWSON RETURNED FROM the subway station to his apartment building an hour later. Cradled in one arm was a brown paper bag that contained a bottle of whiskey, a foil-wrapped corned beef sandwich and a folded copy of the *Daily World*. He had bought the tabloid newspaper on impulse. He hadn't purchased an honest-to-God, printed-on-dead-trees newspaper in years, especially the *Daily World*. He hadn't seen the need. He spent every waking moment on a computer and found whatever news he needed there. Besides, most days, when he looked at a newspaper, he just got angry all over again, about Jimmy.

He climbed the dingy stairwell, lit by a pair of exposed light-bulbs that hung from the ceiling, to his apartment. He didn't want to think about Jimmy, didn't want to think about Jennifer Davis and her worldwide crusade. All he wanted was to down a couple of Irish coffees, eat his sandwich and tune out for a while. Not for the first time, his thoughts traveled to the Walther hidden in his top dresser drawer. Put one through the head and tune out forever. He dismissed the idea immediately. Sure, blowing out his brains may provide sweet relief for him, but it gave no guarantees that Yezhov would leave his family alone. The bastard struck Lawson as vindictive and psychotic enough to wipe out his kin simply for the sake of doing it, to feel like he'd won.

To hell with it, he thought. He'd drink and maybe with a couple of belts in him, he'd change his mind, and the Walther might look better to him.

Standing before his apartment door, he fumbled in his pockets for his keys.

By the time he'd unlocked the door, he was thinking maybe he'd forego the Irish coffee and have a couple of snorts of whiskey. Once he stepped through the door and into his apartment, he turned, and closed and locked the door.

He turned again to head for the kitchen, but halted in his tracks and inhaled sharply. The grocery bag nearly slipped from his grasp. A man leaned against the jamb of the door leading into the kitchen, arms crossed over his chest. The man stared at Lawson with his heavy-lidded, pale green eyes. The gaze seemed lifeless and had struck Lawson previously as somehow reptilian.

"Mikoyan, what the hell are you doing here?" Lawson demanded.

The man ignored him. "You dropped off the package as instructed?"

"I did your damn dirty work, yeah."

The slit that passed for the man's mouth twisted into a cold smile. "I never should have doubted you."

"Look," Lawson said, "I don't want any trouble. I did what you asked. Now leave me alone. Understand?"

"I'll leave you alone when I am finished with you. Do *you* understand?"

A cough sounded from deeper inside the apartment. Lawson's brows furrowed and he glanced through the door that led from his entryway into the kitchen. He saw a man, brown hair marbled with golden highlights, standing in the kitchen, an unlit cigarette perched between his lips. A tattoo of a snake poked out from under the right sleeve of the man's shirt, wound its way down his arm before the body widened into a top view of the serpent's head depicted on the back of the man's hand. Farther inside the apartment, he heard the murmur of the television, accompanied by the occasional guffaws of an unseen man and a prerecorded laugh track.

"Meet your new roommates," Mikoyan said.

"Like I said—"

"You don't want any trouble. Right. That's why you began working with this woman. What does she call herself? Nightingale?"

"I had my reasons."

"Your brother."

Lawson turned his gaze from Mikoyan and studied the store logo, a griffin, printed in red ink on the grocery sack.

"I don't want to go over this."

"I do. You might find it instructive. He was killed in Moscow, right? Car bomb."

"Damn it," Lawson growled.

"Government never found the killers. Correct?"

Lawson bent at the knees and set the grocery bag on the linoleum floor. When he stood back up, his fingers had curled into fists and the knuckles cocked on his hips. His mouth always had been faster than his brain, but even more so when he was angry. The rage roiling within him seared his insides like white-hot phosphorous. He thought longingly of the Walther in his room, fully focused on opening a third eye on the Russian's forehead.

Instead, he stood his ground and opened his mouth.

"You know damn well what happened to Jimmy. He was writing about a Russian crime boss. He was a day, maybe two, from finishing the story. He left work. He was supposed to have dinner with his fiancée—who killed herself later, by the way. He climbed into his car, turned the key. The car blew the fuck up. Remember now?"

Lawson paused a second, then continued. Adrenaline coursed through him, caused his limbs to tremor with rage.

"The rat bastards who publish the *Daily World* squashed the story and eventually closed the Moscow bureau. Blamed it on budget cuts. But we know the real reason, don't we, Mikoyan? Poor, idealistic Jimmy died for no damn reason. The authorities—" he practically spat the last word "—claimed they couldn't find the killer. That's in spite of all the evidence they had, including Jimmy's notes and recorded interviews, all of which they seized and not, coincidentally, lost later. There, Mikoyan, there's your damn story. Happy?"

"Yet, you teamed up with the woman."

"No shit, I was there when it happened."

"You could have worked for Yezhov. Someone with your skills, he would have snapped you up immediately."

"They killed my brother, you damned psychopath!"

"Yet here you are, still without justice. All your brains and talent. You stole money from people. Made them angry. Stuck a thumb in their eye. But the assassin, he or she is still free, right? You worked with this woman and you got nothing for it. Congratulations."

Mikoyan pulled his shoulder away from the doorjamb, brought himself fully erect. He uncrossed his arms, let them hang loose at his sides and stared down at Lawson. The British man stared up into the other man's hollow eyes and his self-righteous anger cooled into fear. When he swallowed, he noticed his throat felt dry.

The Russian's voice suddenly turned bright. "But you have left all that behind you now, haven't you?"

"You're a bastard," Lawson muttered.

"And you're lucky," Mikoyan said, "to still be drawing breath. If it had been up to me——" He gave a slight shrug and left the statement unfinished. "But it's not up to me. Yezhov wants you alive. At least until we see whether that stupid bitch goes and picks up the phone. Once she takes the phone, we can track her wherever she goes. But until that happens, I want you to wait here with my friends. Consider them your friends now, too."

Mikoyan brushed past Lawson and headed for the door. On the way, he knelt down, reached inside the grocery sack, drew out the folded newspaper. Standing erect, he unfolded it and scanned the front page for a couple of seconds. Making a disgusted sound, he tossed it aside and the pages scattered over the floor.

"Never liked this damn rag," he said. "One less reporter could only make the world a better place."

Before Lawson could reply, the other man was out the door and gone.

7

Bolan's mobile phone buzzed. He pulled it from inside his jacket and put it to his ear.

"Go," he said.

"Good news," Kurtzman said, "I may have a lead."

"That would be nice," Bolan said, "since I have nothing."

"The phone the police found? The one the Nightingale apparently left behind? It turned out to be an intelligence gold mine. I'm not sure they even know what they have right now. A lot of their stuff is fragments. But once I fed it into my own programs and started building links, I came up with some good stuff."

"Nice of them to share the information," Bolan said dryly.

"I meant to ask, but hated to trouble them. Fortunately, they were good enough to leave the data in a place where I could find it."

"Behind firewalls in supposedly secure servers."

"Exactly. Hey, do you want to hear what I found or what?"

"Give."

"Gladly. The phone was purchased at a convenience store in Bayswater. Nothing special about the store. They deal in cell phones, beer, cigarettes, all of it legal, nearly all of it mundane as hell."

"So she bought it there?"

"No, I said they were purchased there, but not by a woman. I'll get to that. Just hang tight. The last phone, the one the Nightingale used, it was the first piece, or the last piece, depending on how you want to look at it, in a series of cutouts. This guy bought the phones and the minutes, then he'd forward the calls from one to another phone, then a third phone. Primitive tradecraft, but effective, nonetheless."

Kurtzman paused and Bolan heard the click of fingers pounding against a keyboard. "So I gathered the phone numbers stored in the phone, backtracked them, hacked into the phone company records and gathered credit card data. The cards were all fake or stolen, by the way. This clown has broken some serious international laws."

"Like hacking bank and government computers."

"Don't judge me," Kurtzman said, a smile audible in his voice. "I have right on my side. Regardless, his tradecraft is pretty good. If I didn't have all the, um, access I have here at the Farm, it would have taken longer to piece it together. Since technically we don't exist, I technically didn't hack into anybody's computer. But if I had, I would have traced the purchases and figured out that several of them were denied by credit card companies. That triggered the shop owners to call the police, who were given surveillance film of the person buying the phones."

"His face visible?"

"Yeah."

"So much for the good tradecraft."

"Yeah, he pretty much screwed the pooch at that point. Figuratively speaking at least."

"We hope."

"I had the cyber team work with the photos, highlight his face, run it through all the databases, blah, blah, blah. We got a hit. Guy's name is Nigel Lawson. Apparently, several years ago, he tried hacking into computers of the Moscow police. More to the point, he succeeded in hacking their computers and stealing a bunch of investigative records."

"Not to satisfy his morbid curiosity I assume."

Another flurry of clicking on the keyboard, followed by Kurtzman clucking his tongue. Bolan assumed he was reading. After several seconds, he spoke.

"Not even close. Apparently, he had a brother who was murdered in Moscow. The investigation wasn't moving at the speed he wanted, so he decided to take matters into his own hands. The first step was breaking into the police computer, which apparently wasn't a huge stretch for our friend. The Russian police tracked him back to England and demanded the Brits extradite him to Russia to stand trial. To its credit, the British government told their counterparts in Moscow to bite the queen's ass, again figuratively speaking."

"Thanks for the clarification."

"It gets better," Kurtzman said. "The Brits apparently let Nigel sweat it for a little bit. They threatened him with extradition, even though they had no intention of following through. They told him if he cooperated, maybe they could help him."

"Cooperation being?"

"He worked with MI5 and MI6, showed them how he hacked the Russian computers. In exchange, British intelligence let him waddle back to his mother's basement, where he could eat pork rinds and drink sugary soda by the case. And here's the best part. His case officer? Your friend Damon Blair."

"The analyst?"

"None other. Apparently, he used to be an operations guy before he switched to analysis. No undercover work or anything. Just meeting with academic sources, interrogating defectors with computer backgrounds, that sort of thing."

Bolan sipped his coffee and continued listening.

Kurtzman continued, "And Blair also lost a daughter years ago. See a pattern?"

Bolan scowled. "Yeah."

"I guess he neglected to mention all this?"

"Yeah again," the soldier said.

"One other thing. Another mindblower. I got a copy of the prints on the recovered phone. Apparently, it's the first time—at least that anyone knows about—where one of the Nightingale's phones have been recovered. I have no doubt she's burned through a ton of them. But she obviously did a good job disposing of them along the way, too.

"This time was different, obviously, with people gunning for her. She dropped the phone when she fled. The Brits were able to get a partial print from it, which I in turn snatched from them. Damn good thing, too. I went back a couple of hours later and the damn thing was gone from the system. Wiped clean. My guess is, if you checked with the London Metropolitan Police, the phone's gone, too."

"Either they handed it over to the spooks," Bolan said, "or one of the spy agencies snagged it on their own."

"Yeah, yeah," Kurtzman replied. "But that's a sideshow. Here's the interesting piece. The prints at first came back as nothing, but that's because I was putting it through a criminal database. Then I remembered what Blair told you, about Jennifer Davis. I broke into her old employer's system, found the prints she submitted when she was first hired at the bank. Voilá! I had a match."

Bolan's eyes narrowed and he unconsciously gripped the phone harder.

"Jennifer Davis?" he asked.

"Jennifer Davis."

"So, she's alive."

"Either that or someone's carrying around a dead woman's finger and poking things with it. If so, this is a whole new level of weird."

Bolan allowed himself a tight smile.

"Let's stick with the more plausible scenario," he said. "She's alive. That brings us back to Blair and Lawson."

"It's possible Blair really thought she was dead. Two analysts can look at the same information and come to totally different conclusions."

"Or he knows she's alive and is covering her tracks for her."

"Because he sympathizes with her."

"Right."

USING A CREDIT CARD, Bolan jimmied open the front door of Lawson's apartment building and climbed the stairs. Kurtzman had given him the man's address before they ended their phone call. The soldier's hand drifted inside his jacket. He wrapped his fingers around the weapon's grip, but kept it holstered.

On his way to the apartment building, the soldier had tried

calling Blair at his office at MI5's headquarters, but got his voice mail. A call to the man's cell phone produced the same result. Bolan decided against leaving a message. He knew the other man likely would see and recognize Bolan's telephone number among his missed calls. He didn't mind if Blair knew he called. But the Executioner was suspicious of his newfound ally and Bolan didn't want his voice to betray that fact.

The Executioner reached Lawson's door, started to knock, but hesitated. He had circled the building a couple of times, taken some time to watch for obvious surveillance and matched what he saw with satellite photos that Kurtzman had sent to his phone.

Nothing seemed amiss. But it was hard to know for certain as he was in unfamiliar territory.

Bolan heard the creak of a doorknob turning. A glance over his shoulder revealed the door to the apartment next to Lawson's swinging inward.

The soldier tensed, but relaxed almost immediately as he saw an elderly woman shuffle through the door and pull it shut behind her. Her frail form wrapped in a black coat, head covered by a matching scarf, she looked up at Bolan, who acknowledged her with a nod. Clutching her purse to her side, she shuffled past the soldier and headed for the stairs.

"Just buy 'em and get the hell out," she muttered.

"Excuse me?"

The woman looked at Bolan with a panicked expression. He stepped up behind her and gently set a hand on her shoulder to stop her. Her shoulder twitched in fear at his touch.

"It's okay," Bolan said. "I'm with the police."

The woman pivoted toward him, the soles of her shoes scraping against the floor.

"Where's your badge?"

Bolan pulled out his fake Justice Department credentials and flashed them at the lady, not giving her a chance to study them.

"You said, 'Just buy 'em and get out.'"

"No, I said get the hell out," she responded, not missing a beat.

Bolan stifled a grin. "Sure. Why did you say that?"

She gestured at Lawson's door with a bony finger.

"That boy there? Nigel? He's lived here for years. Quiet. He'll open a door for you, carry your groceries upstairs. He drinks, but he's quiet. No women coming over. No drugs. None of that."

The woman looked side to side before staring again at Bolan. "That was until this week."

"What happened this week?"

She licked her lips and gestured at the door with a nod. "Then they came."

"Who's they?"

"The Russians. The damn Russians have been here all week. They knocked on my door, asking me questions. I slammed the door in their faces. Told them to go to hell. Told them I didn't like the bloody Commies twenty years ago, and I still don't."

Bolan considered pointing out that the Soviet Union had dissolved decades ago, but decided to save the lecture in geopolitics for another visit.

"What kind of questions were they asking?"

She hesitated.

Bolan mustered up his most earnest look. "Please," he said. "It's important."

"Wanted to know where he was, when he'd be home. All sorts of questions. None of it was their damn business."

She shifted on her feet uncomfortably and leaned a hip against a nearby rail.

"At first, I thought they were harassing Nigel. But then I saw them coming and going. All of them."

"Today?"

"You deaf? Yes, today. In and out the door. Doing God knows what."

"How many are there?"

"Three. The tall one—he looks like the walking dead—left an hour ago. The other two are still there, I think." She leaned forward, scrunched up her face as though she'd tasted something awful. "One of them had tattoos on him, too."

She studied Bolan, apparently gauging his reaction. He hoped his face reflected the requisite amount of shock.

"You could hear them?"

She shook her head. "Can't hear nothing. Place is a century old. Walls are brick. Doors are heavy wood. That's why I stay here. I don't like people nosing in my business." She stopped and took a breath. "But I saw 'em go in," she said, "and haven't seen 'em come out."

"Maybe you missed them?"

"I don't miss anything."

Bolan nodded.

"I think they're selling drugs in there," the woman said. "All those Russians, they're all in the mob. I know that. You know that. Everyone knows that."

Bolan hadn't known that, but nodded again anyway.

"Thanks for the help," he said.

She gestured dismissively with her hand.

"Just do something about all these damn Russians, eh? Place is going to hell. Fix it."

"Consider it fixed, ma'am."

LAWSON WAS HIS third drink into the whiskey when he decided to fix his situation.

After Mikoyan had left, he'd gathered up the newspaper and his groceries and moved to the kitchen. The Russians apparently considered him beneath their notice. The one who'd been watching television—a stubble-faced guy with a rangy build and long, gray hair—came into the kitchen long enough to take half of Lawson's sandwich and his bag of chips before returning to the living room to zone out in front of the television.

Lawson had eaten the other half of his sandwich. That and the whiskey had formed a nice warm spot in his belly. A pleasant light-headedness had come over him.

He looked at the second thug, the one covered in tattoos. The guy stood in front of the kitchen window, backside resting on the sill. A rectangular phone in his hand demanded all his attention. The unlit cigarette still protruding from his lips, he stared down at the rectangular mobile phone. His thumbs moved up and down like little pistons.

"You texting someone?" he asked.

The Russian glanced up. "Yeah," he said. "Your brother."

His eyes returned to the phone's screen.

"Ask him if your grandma still gives the best blow jobs in Heaven," Lawson said.

The man raised his head and glared at Lawson. He tensed himself for a confrontation, but the thug shook his head and returned to his phone. After a few seconds, Lawson rose up from the chair, setting a hand on the tabletop to steady himself.

The man covered in tattoos looked up at him again.

"Gotta take a piss," Lawson said, slurring his words more than necessary. "And, no, you can't come in and hold it for me."

The other guy glared at Lawson, but made no threatening moves.

The Englishman lumbered through the living room. When he stepped between the gray-haired Russian and the television, the guy looked up at him. "Where the hell you going?"

"Gotta take a dump," Lawson murmured.

The man pointed back through the kitchen. "Bathroom's through there."

"I need a book," Lawson said. "You know, those thick things with all the words."

Like the other guard, this one with the stubble just glared at Lawson, but made no move to stop him.

Once inside the bedroom, he scuffed his feet against the floor. The way he saw it, the more noise he made, the less attention he'd garner. When he reached his dresser, he slowly pulled open the top drawer, reached a hand inside and felt around for the Walther. When his fingertips brushed against it, he grasped the weapon and drew it from the drawer.

"What's taking so long?" a voice said from behind.

Normally, Lawson would have froze, but the alcohol seemed to lubricate his movements. Turning his head, he leveled the pistol at the gray-haired man and fired.

The pistol's report in such a confined space seemed deafening to Lawson. A small, red hole opened on the Russian's shoulder and he stumbled backward. Lawson walked toward the guy, ready to line up another shot. The fallen man brought around his own gun, a large-bore, silver revolver, and fired it. Lawson's gun cracked in the same instant. The round opened a hole in the man's throat.

The impact from the large bullet had shoved Lawson off his feet. He'd fallen to the ground and was leaning against the bed. The shock wore off almost immediately and he felt white-hot pain lancing through his midsection. He placed a hand over the wound in a vain attempt to staunch the bleeding.

Footsteps thudded outside the door. He guessed the other thug was coming. Once he saw what Lawson had done, he'd likely kill him. It was at that moment, he realized he'd lost his pistol, leaving him injured and defenseless.

EVEN THROUGH THE brick walls, Bolan heard the gunfire. The Desert Eagle was holstered in the small of his back. He reached under his jacket and unsheathed it. He quickly tried the door but, as expected, found it was locked. He raised the pistol and fired two rounds through the lock.

The door swung inward and Bolan went through the door.

He heard someone yelling in Russian from farther inside the apartment. He moved quickly through the kitchen and into the living room, where he saw the man with the tattoos kneeling next to an older man who was sprawled on the floor.

With his right hand, he was shaking the man and yelling. In his left hand, he held a large silver automatic that he was pointing into another room that Bolan couldn't see into.

The soldier raised the Desert Eagle, centered its muzzle on the guy's back and fired. Thunder pealed in the apartment and the .44-caliber round lanced through the man's spine, killing him instantly. The guy pitched forward. Bolan walked past him and into the bedroom at his left.

He saw Lawson sitting on the floor, back propped against the edge of the bed. A dark stain was spreading over the fabric that covered Lawson's ample midsection. His breath was coming in ragged gasps. A blood-covered hand was clutched over a wound.

Bolan saw a pistol on the floor just out of Lawson's reach and kicked it away before kneeling next to the guy.

"Nigel?"

The guy turned and looked at Bolan.

"Who?"

"I'm a friend," Bolan said. "Friend of yours. Friend of Jennifer's."

"Fuck."

"What?" Bolan said.

"Jennifer."

"What about her?"

"Terrible?" he replied. "Did something terrible…"

"What did you do?"

"Cell phone. Gave it to her. They can track her."

"Who?"

"Yezhov."

By now, Bolan had grabbed a folded T-shirt and was pressing it against Lawson's wound. But the guy looked pale, his eyes unfocused, his breath unsteady.

"I'll call for help," Bolan said.

"Forget it," Lawson said. "Tell, tell, tell her I'm sorry. Coming for family."

Pushing aside the bed, the soldier stretched Lawson out on the floor. A final death rattle escaped the guy's lungs and he slipped into death.

8

Jennifer Davis threaded her way through the crush of people populating the dance club.

The place throbbed with the pounding rhythms of a techno-dance song. Cigarette smoke and artificial fog hung in the air, stung her eyes. She swept her eyes over the club's interior. She'd received an urgent text message from Lawson, asking her to come here. That he'd asked to meet her had surprised her. Lawson wasn't the dance-club type. Had he gotten cold feet or, worse, had something happened to him?

Her hand reached down to the purse she carried and unzipped it. As she did, the last song faded and the intro to a new one blared through the sound system. Immediately, she recognized the sampled guitar riffs and preprogrammed drumbeats. Grief squeezed her heart and spurred a dull ache in her throat.

Her sister, Jessica, had loved clubs, had loved to dance. As young women, they'd spent countless hours dancing in clubs. As time had moved on, though, the girls' nights on the town had diminished more with each passing year. Jennifer had her career, and so did Jessica, of course, but her attention increasingly was focused on her marriage.

Davis continued walking through the London club, but her surroundings faded away, replaced by the Blind Lemon, a New York dance club. Seated across from Jessica. A waitress had just set a stem glass on a cocktail napkin on the table in front of Jennifer before bustling away. Unlike previous outings, where the crush of daily living increasingly had forced them to schedule time together, this meeting was impromptu. Jessica had called just after lunch. She had important news. Could they meet for drinks? No, she wouldn't say any more. Just show up!

Davis still could feel the excitement that fluttered in her stomach that afternoon. She knew her sister had been trying for months to get pregnant. She had hoped that was the news.

A glass filled with a clear liquid and a slice of lime was on the table in front of her sister. Jennifer had nodded at the glass.

"Gin and tonic? Since when do you drink gin?"

Her sister, already smiling, shook her head.

"Not gin," she said. "Club soda."

"You're not drinking."

"Can't."

Her sister's smile widened and tears welled up in her eyes.

Davis had screamed and jumped from her stool. Her twin did likewise. They threw their arms around one another and Jessica whispered in her sister's ear, "You're going to be an auntie."

She had started to cry.

For a moment, she wasn't aware of the strong fingers wrapped around her biceps. When she realized there was a big man with ice-blue eyes and close-cropped black hair standing next to her, it startled her. Over the years, she'd gained an almost infallible sixth sense capable of picking up on danger. She tried to jerk her arm free, but he kept his grip firm.

"Jennifer," the man said, "we need to talk. I'm here to help."

DAVIS PULLED HER ARM away again. This time, Bolan let it go. She took a step back. He held up his hands, palms facing her, in mock surrender.

"We're here to help," he repeated.

"Bull," she said. "I don't even know you. Why should I trust you?"

Because I'm your only chance. The words careened through Bolan's mind, but he didn't utter them. He knew the woman had been on the run for years, alternatively plundering and running from bad guys. Within the past couple of days, she'd come dan-

gerously close to dying. Though obviously a brave woman, she
was scared and in over her head.

"Nigel sent us," Bolan said.

"Now I know you're lying," she responded, her disbelief audible in her voice. "Nigel wouldn't send anyone for me. He'd
come for me himself."

"He couldn't," Bolan said. "Not tonight. I was the one who
sent the text message."

"Where is he?"

"He's dead," Bolan said.

It was hard to tell in the club's lighting, but Bolan thought he
saw the woman's face turn pale. Her hand flew up and she rested
her palm on her chest.

"How do you know?"

"We were there when it happened," Bolan said.

Her eyes narrowed. "You mean you killed him." Her hand
drifted downward and her fingertips slipped into the right hip
pocket of her overcoat.

Bolan knew what she was thinking. He shook his head.

"You don't want to do that," Bolan said. "We're here to help
you."

Her hand froze and her lips pressed into a tight line. She studied Bolan for a stretched second before she drew her fingers from
her pocket and let her arm hang at her side.

Bolan moved his hand slowly and flipped open a black-leather
badge case. The card identified him as Matt Cooper, an agent
with the Justice Department. She studied it for a few minutes.

"Matt Cooper, huh?" she said.

"Yes."

"Are you here to arrest me?"

"Do I have to?"

She fell silent again.

"Look," Bolan said, "you can't do this. It's bigger than you."

Her features softened, the deep furrows in her forehead melt-
ing away. One corner of her mouth twitched. She examined the
DOJ credentials once more, then nodded slowly.

"Okay," she said, "let's go."

OUTSIDE THE CLUB, the black BMW sport-utility vehicle idled at the curb, black-tinted windows impenetrable, headlights extinguished. Parked behind the SUV was McCarter's Jaguar, also running, with the Phoenix Force commander sitting behind the wheel. When he saw Bolan, he acknowledged the American with a nod.

"Friends of yours?" Davis asked.

"Some of the few," Bolan said.

He opened the rear passenger's-side door and gestured for Davis to climb into the SUV. He watched as she peered inside, hesitated for a few seconds before climbing in. Bolan shut the door behind her and walked around the back of the vehicle to the rear door on the driver's side. He barely had settled into his seat when he extended his right hand toward her, palm facing up.

"I need your cell phone," he said.

"What?"

"Your phone," he said. "Give it to me."

She opened her mouth to reply.

"Please," Bolan said. "And your tablet computer."

Her lips pressed into a hard line and she studied Bolan's face. "This is crap," she said, finally. Her hand lashed out and took hold of the door handle. She pulled up on it, but found it wouldn't open. She pulled a couple more times and tried to work the locking mechanism. She whipped her head back toward Bolan. Anger flashed in her eyes.

"What the hell is this?" she demanded.

"The phone," Bolan said.

"What the hell? The door's locked. You want me to give up my phone, my computer. I thought I was coming voluntarily."

"You did come voluntarily."

"And now I'm locked in your car."

"If you were a prisoner," Bolan said, "I would have taken your gun. The one on your right hip, hidden by the hem of your coat."

Her eyes automatically flicked to her right, then snapped back in Bolan's direction. Bolan wondered for a moment whether she might deny the gun's existence. Instead, she heaved a sigh and her shoulders drooped. She reached into her jacket, drew out the phone and passed it to Bolan. The soldier took it from her with one hand and with the index finger of his other hand, punched the button that opened his window. The window lowered. McCarter stepped into view and Bolan passed the phone through the window to him and closed the window.

"Your phone was bugged," Bolan said. "They've been tracking you by GPS for the past hour or so, at least."

Even as Bolan spoke, Grimaldi dropped the SUV into gear and eased it into traffic.

The Executioner saw that Davis was looking at him—almost seemed to be looking through him. Finally, she shook her head from side to side, slowly, as though refusing to let reality sink in.

"Nigel left the phone for me. He wouldn't do that to me. We've known each other for years."

"He did do it."

"But why? Why would he want to do that?" she asked.

"I don't think he wanted to."

"You're not making any sense."

"He has family in the States?" Bolan asked.

"California. So?"

"So, the people hunting you figured it out. Once they had your name and Nigel's name, they did some legwork and realized he had people close to him. They hunted him down. They told him they wanted him to play on their side and made sure he knew that refusing to do so would be harmful to the health of a lot of people."

She raked her fingers through her hair, wrapped them around the back of her neck and squeezed it gently. "He had to choose between them and me?"

"Yes," Bolan said.

"He had to choose them, of course. All those lives."

"Right."

"Because he knew me, helped me."

"To a point."

She turned her head and stared at Bolan.

"To a point? Not to a point," she said. "Those people would have died because they were close to Nigel. He was close to me, helping me. This isn't rocket science. His family members were going to get killed because of me."

"They were going to get killed because the people you are fighting are bad people. They have no problem going after innocent people if it gets them some leverage. That's not your fault."

"But—"

"But they wouldn't go after Nigel's family if they weren't trying to get you? Agreed."

"I never meant for any of this to happen."

"Of course you didn't."

She drew in a sharp breath.

"Shit," she said, "I have family, too. If they know I am alive—"

Bolan cut her off. "It's been dealt with."

"How?" she asked, eyeing Bolan warily.

"We've dispatched protective teams to your family, at least the most immediate relatives—parents, aunts, uncles. We put out alerts to the hometown cops where you have other close relatives. You have first cousins in Cleveland and Dayton, right?"

She nodded.

"I don't think anyone's going any deeper than that," Bolan said. "At least not right now. If it starts to look like we need to worry, we can have protective details moved into those other places, too."

"How quickly?"

"I have connections. My connections have even bigger connections. Speed won't be a problem."

"It's not a permanent fix."

"It's enough for now. Don't worry, I won't leave any loose ends hanging around."

"My family, do they know I'm alive?"

Bolan shook his head. "We're telling them it has to do with some associates of Khallad Mukhtar, the man who killed your sister. Hopefully, they won't ask too many other questions."

Bolan noticed the corners of her lips were turned down and she'd returned to studying her fingernails. He guessed she was conflicted, wanting her family to know she was alive, to have at least a moment's connection with them. At the same time, she knew full well that letting them know she still walked the earth could make them into targets for every hood wanting to settle a score with her.

At least on some level, the Executioner understood her quandary. As far as the public was concerned, Mack Samuel Bolan as such had died years ago. His brother, Johnny, had been a boy when Bolan had launched his Everlasting War. Now a full-grown man working as a private detective, the younger Bolan occasionally called on his older brother for help.

"As long as I am around," she said, "they're not going to leave my family, my friends alone. I knew that from the start. It's why I faked my own death."

"Believe me, I understand why you've done the things you have," he said.

"What? Stealing from crooks and killers? I don't apologize for that."

"Good, you shouldn't."

She silently stared at Bolan for several seconds. It seemed she was searching for something, though Bolan couldn't guess what it was.

"You're different."

"Tell me about it."

"No, really. You're not judging me for what I've done."

"True."

"You're not a cop."

"Never said I was," Bolan said simply.

"You said you're with the Justice Department."

"I did."

"But you're not an FBI agent, a cop."

"No."

"Jesus, you make no sense."

"Hope you like your men mysterious," Grimaldi called over his shoulder.

"*Like*'s not a word I'd use with you two."

"And she goes for the jugular," the pilot said.

"Here's the thing," Bolan said. "I think you ought to keep

doing what you've been doing. Just come in from the wilds and do it with government cover. Stop living on the run."

"I can't keep doing this," she said. "Not if it's going to put my family in harm's way. Now that people know I am alive, they will always have a score to settle."

"Like I said, I get it. I understand why you wanted revenge. Why you concocted the whole house explosion to cover your trail. You didn't do that for yourself, did you?" he said. "I get the stress of living on the run. Trust me, I get all of it. Here's the thing, I can offer you an easier way. It won't necessarily be easy, just easier."

She nodded.

"We can go back to the States, set you up somewhere to do your work. I'm not sure where, what agency you'd work for. That's secondary, frankly. The important thing is you wouldn't have to run anymore."

"What about my family?"

Bolan shrugged. "We'll take care of them, don't worry. Like I said, we already have people moving right now to make sure they'll be okay."

"People? Like you?"

"Something like that."

"Will I be able to see them again?" she asked.

"No," Bolan said, "you won't."

Her cheeks flushed red. "Why the hell not? If I'm giving all this up, why can't I see them?"

"We both already know the answer to that, Jennifer."

She inhaled deeply, let it out in a long sigh.

"Because I'll always be a risk to them."

Bolan nodded. "Unfortunately, yes."

"I guess I chose this path."

Bolan shrugged again. "Maybe. Maybe it chose you. I'm not smart enough to know that. What I do know is you're already walking it. It's too late to change now. You're in too deep."

"Okay," she said, "what happens to me?"

"You stay underground, at least as far as your old life is concerned," Bolan said. "I'm guessing you'll get set up with a new identity. Maybe give you a cover job somewhere so you can continue your work without having to look over your shoulder all the time. You'll be alone and disconnected, at least from your old ties."

"But I'm already that."

"Exactly."

Davis studied the fingernails of her left hand for several moments.

"When do we leave?"

"Tonight," Bolan said. "We have a jet waiting."

Davis shook her head.

"Not tonight," she said.

"Excuse me?"

"I need to stay until tomorrow."

"We can't—"

"I came here for a reason," she said. "To London, I mean. Think about it. If I really wanted to fall off the grid, there are a lot of places better than London. I can think of half a dozen African countries where I could get lost. That's just for starters. I came here because I wanted to be here."

"Because of your sister."

She nodded. "Yes, my sister. Her husband. My niece."

"I didn't realize you had a niece."

"My sister was pregnant when she was killed. Look, I'll spare you my sob story. I've already replayed that movie a million times in my head. It never ends any differently. I don't plan to drag it out for you and your friend here to see."

"Fair enough," Bolan said.

"But I'm not going anywhere until tomorrow. It's the anniversary of her death and I want to go to the bombing site, the train station, and leave some roses. Let me do that, and I'll be happy to go back to the States with you. Tell me no and I'm not going anywhere with you."

Bolan considered the woman's words. His gut told him it was a bad play. The sooner they got out of London, returned her to American soil and handed Davis over to Brognola, the better off they'd all be. She could take on a new life. Bolan could move ahead to the next mission.

He looked at her. The set of her jaw, the resolve in her eyes, told him she'd already made up her mind. He could try to force her to go, but that would only make it more likely that she'd bolt once they reached Washington. If Davis did that, the whole mission would be a failure.

"Okay," Bolan said, regret washing over him as he uttered the word. "It's late. We have a safe house. We stay there. You get a shower and some coffee. We go to the bombing site first thing in the morning. Then we get the hell out of the country."

THE SAFE HOUSE WAS a two-story duplex several blocks from the Thames River. Bolan poured coffee into three mugs. He slid one across the counter to Grimaldi. With a nod, the pilot took the cup, strode to one of the windows and peered outside at an oppressive rain that had begun falling on the city. Bolan picked up the other two and walked to the round dining table where Davis sat. He set the coffee in front of her and she thanked him.

He seated himself across the table from her. He tested the coffee, found it was too hot and set the cup on the table. Davis curled an index finger through the ring on her cup and stared at her coffee.

"Why's Yezhov after you?" Bolan asked.

"Didn't Nigel tell you?"

"Said he didn't know."

"Nigel went to his grave a liar. He knew why. I told him. I wonder what else he lied about?"

Bolan shook his head. "Doesn't matter at this point. What didn't he tell me?"

She scooted back in the chair, drew up her right ankle and tucked it beneath her left thigh.

"I didn't just take his money, Yezhov's money, I mean. I got hold of some other files."

"What files?"

"I'll get to that. Occasionally, when I hack into a system, I vacuum out whatever else I can find. A lot of it ranges from mundane to downright disgusting, homemade snuff films and other crazy stuff. There are some horrible people in the world."

"I'm hiding my shock."

"Yeah, you strike me as someone who's seen it all."

"Seen it all two or three times over."

"I'm sorry," she said. "That's no way to live."

"We all make our choices. Tell me what you found."

"Right. A lot of the stuff on Yezhov's computer was pedestrian. I mean it was an intelligence gold mine. Lists of shell companies and accounts. It was all valuable, but none of it surprised me. I kept digging, though, figuring I might find a horse underneath all the manure."

"And you did."

"More like a bear, a very angry bear. Yezhov's up to his neck in extremely bad stuff. Not the usual organized-crime stuff, either—though there's plenty of that. But this is a lot more sinister."

"Explain."

"Well, for starters, he's not working alone. He's got a network of people, all Russian, some are government officials, others work in the private sector. Bunch of pilferers. You couldn't fit a piece of paper between the government and the private-sector people. They use the government as their own personal ATM and prop up the government officials with bribes and gifts." She took a sip of coffee. Holding the cup several inches from her face, she stared into it.

"Group calls itself the Sindikat," she said. "It's loosely organized. Yezhov's the top dog, though. From what I gather, he wields a lot of power. He owns a shipping conglomerate, air transport, all sorts of things. He has a figurehead president who runs the company, gives it an air of legitimacy."

"Legitimacy?"

"Yezhov was big in Russian intelligence, a real rising star, according to my sources."

"Sources? Like Nigel?"

"Better than Nigel. Much better. A couple of former spies who are still plugged in when it comes to Russia and Asia."

"These spies, do they have names?"

"Yes."

A few seconds passed. "And they are?" Bolan asked.

"My secret."

"I can't check their authenticity if you don't give me the names."

"I can live with that," Davis said icily.

Bolan drew in a breath, exhaled slowly. Should he push the issue? Not yet, he decided. With the help of Stony Man Farm, he could verify a lot of the information without pushing Davis too hard. He was trying to establish some rapport, not prod her into bolting.

"Fair enough," he said. "But let's skip the build up and get to the punch line."

"You heard of something called Keyhole Twelve?"

Bolan thought about it for a moment and realized it didn't mean anything to him. He shook his head.

"You've heard of the original Keyhole satellite program?"

Grimaldi spoke without looking away from the window. "Cold War satellite program."

"Exactly," she said. "There were at least a couple versions of the Keyhole satellite that the public knows about. We used them to spy on the Soviets and their nuclear programs. Publicly, that's all the Keyhole ever was."

Grimaldi turned away from the window. "Publicly?"

"There was another, parallel program. It was called the Sentry Satellite. It had a fancy, twelve-word name, too. But the short version was Sentry. It was a satellite killer. The way it was explained to me is that the original Sentry satellites focused on jamming techniques. The idea was to cripple the satellites without leaving fingerprints. They just suddenly—" she snapped her fingers "—went black. But they were still there, so it got chalked up to faulty designs or faulty manufacturing. I don't understand all the technology, but they were able to make it look like the satellites just went belly up."

She shifted in her chair.

"Over the years, they merged the two programs together, added and dropped names. Eventually, they kept Keyhole as the umbrella name for both programs. Publicly Keyhole was dead, old technology. But they decided to keep it internally. It sounded less threatening, like a spy satellite."

"Which it no longer was."

"No," Davis said. "The country has plenty of eyes in the sky, especially with private companies getting into the act. This thing is pure destructive power. It uses directed energy—"

"A.k.a. laser," Grimaldi said.

"Sorry for the jargon. Yeah, it's a laser. A powerful laser capable of taking out satellites with the press of a couple of buttons. The U.S. has a half dozen flying in space. We'd have more, but they're expensive as hell. Gets too unwieldy to hide black projects once they exceed a certain dollar amount."

"But that's good, right?" Grimaldi asked. "At least from our perspective, we have the upper hand."

"Sure, except the Sindikat has placed a couple of spies, high-level egghead types, into the National Geospatial Intelligence Agency, the organization in charge of the program. They fed the Sindikat all kinds of information, particularly on the laser capabilities and ways to link an outside computer into the U.S. system. Yezhov, in turn, has been selling that data back to the Russians. They've been able to gather important design information about the satellites. And they just scored an even bigger coup. They convinced one of the guys to provide the override codes for the satellite controls whenever they ask."

"So even if they change, the Sindikat can get the updated codes."

"Exactly."

"How does Yezhov know that you have all this information?"

"I wondered that, too. Now that Nigel's dead, I guess I have the answer."

"You told him all this?"

"I did."

"Who else knows?"

"My intelligence sources. Remember? The ones I won't name."

"We can't warn them if we don't have their names."

"Nigel wouldn't share the names. Don't look at me that way,

he wouldn't. Not because he's a good guy. He doesn't know the names. I tend to compartmentalize that stuff."

"He doesn't communicate with anyone else in the organization?"

Her brows furrowed. "Just one," she said. "But I didn't tell either one that the other had the information."

"It doesn't matter," Bolan said. "If he assumes that this person knows, or even if he gave up their name, they could be in danger, too."

She brought up her hands, covered her face with them. "Damn, damn, damn. I am so stupid."

"No, you're not," Bolan said. "You trusted someone who seemed to be on your side. He turned on you. It happens."

"Seems to be happening a lot—and quickly."

"Give me the name."

"But—" Her shoulders slumped. "Damn it. Okay, her name's Maxine Young."

"Can you contact her?"

Her expression miserable, she shook her head from side to side. "She's on her way to England tonight. I got a text from her a few hours ago. I guess Nigel called her, told her that I needed her here. I tried calling, but couldn't get through to her. She must be in transit."

9

Maxine Young climbed down the steps of the chartered jet. The chilled air whipping across the tarmac tousled the stray strands of ash-blond hair not tied into a ponytail. A cold drizzle fell on the airport. She looked skyward at the black thunderheads rolling in over the city and scowled.

The strap of her overnight bag, a black leather satchel that she normally kept stored under her bed, was looped over one shoulder. Her purse was slung over the other shoulder. The overnight bag contained a change of clothes, toiletries, a hair dryer and a curling iron. However, sewn into the liner was a fake passport and fake credit cards and several thousand real U.S. dollars. Though retired for some time, she'd kept the bag at the ready, partly from habit and partly from necessity.

Having received Nigel Lawson's call, she was glad she'd prepared for a last-minute trip.

Her emotions were conflicted. She was worried for Davis's safety. After years of working together, the former CIA agent felt as though the younger woman was like a daughter and not just a friend. Even their brief telephone conversations and rare face-to-face meetings filled the void left behind after her husband and son had been killed in Mumbai, India. At the same time, it felt good—damn good, actually—to be back in action again. The excitement fluttering in her stomach felt at once familiar and foreboding, but welcome nonetheless.

She got her passport stamped with no problems, exited the main building and headed for the parking lot Lawson had di-

rected her to. She swept her gaze over the gathered cars until
she found the one she was looking for, a red compact. Walking to the car, she opened the passenger's side, stripped off her
overnight bag and sat it on the floor of the vehicle. Pulling off
her purse, she set it on top of the overnight bag. Resting a hand
on the passenger's seat, she reached across the small car's interior, and felt around below the dashboard. When she found the
lever that opened the trunk, she pulled on it and heard the latch
release in the trunk compartment.

Easing back out of the car, she walked around to the trunk.
Inside it, she found a cardboard box, the flaps held closed with
a piece of masking tape. A logo on the side of the box included
a drawing of a man and woman locked in passion. Underneath
the drawing, written in bold, red letters: Night Moves Magic
Body Oils.

Very classy, Nigel, she thought.

With the tip of a red-lacquered fingernail, she sawed through
the masking tape and peeled back the flaps, half afraid to look
inside. A cloth bundle sat in one corner of the box. She picked it
up, unwrapped it and inside found a SIG-Sauer pistol sheathed
in a holster. Two more ammo clips, bound together with a rub-
ber band, sat in the box, along with a mobile telephone. Undoing
the belt of her overcoat, she peeled back the right side, quickly
slipped a hand beneath the folds of her coat and clipped the holstered weapon to her belt. She slid the magazines into one coat
pocket and the phone into another.

She slammed the trunk closed and she quickly climbed into
the driver's seat. With her left hand, she grabbed the edge of the
sun visor and pulled it down. The keys fell into the waiting palm
of her right hand. The parking-lot ticket also fluttered down. She
set the slip of paper on her left thigh, belted herself in and fired
up the car. Before she put the tiny vehicle into gear, though, she
remembered to power up her cell phone, so she wouldn't miss
any calls.

As she drove, Young tried to recall how long it had been since
she'd visited London. Five years? Six? She honestly couldn't re-

member. Losing her family had turned her life into a cold, gray blur, an unending journey through a barren and uncertain world. Weekends, holidays, anniversaries, all had lost meaning for her. Like the young woman she'd teamed with, the only thing that allowed even the smallest slivers of sunlight into her days was the knowledge that she was fighting the good fight, in most cases for people unable to fight for themselves. A lot of days, that knowledge and the lump of cold rage the killers had shoved into the space once occupied by her heart were the only things powerful enough to push her out of bed and back into life.

Checking the GPS unit on the dashboard, she saw the street she needed was coming up on her right, a couple dozen yards ahead. When she came to the turn, she tapped the brake to slow the car and twisted the steering wheel to the right. She traveled a block down the street, pulled the car up to the curb and parked it, amazed to find a spot so close to her destination.

Grabbing her things, she disembarked from the car and walked another three blocks to her hotel. After the long flight, all she wanted was to take a hot shower, crawl into bed and grab a few hours' sleep before she caught up with Davis.

Truth be told, she would have rather met her immediately, but Lawson had told her that wasn't part of the plan. Davis was nearby and would be in the neighborhood long before they actually rendezvoused, Young had been assured. However, the younger woman had planned to do a little recon around the meeting site beforehand, sweep the place for bugs and make sure Young hadn't picked up any followers.

Young initially had bristled at the notion that she couldn't spot a tail and had told Lawson just that. Ultimately, though, she admitted—to herself at least—that her protégé was practicing good operations security and Young decided to shut up.

She checked into the hotel and requested that a chilled bottle of white wine be sent to her room in thirty minutes. That'd give her enough time to get a quick shower and slip into her pajamas and robe before room service arrived.

She rode the elevator to her room, her eyes scanning her surroundings the whole time. For reasons she couldn't quite pinpoint, she began to feel unsettled. Her mouth was dry and sweat slicked her palms. Was it intuition or just a case of jitters since she'd been out of circulation so long? She guessed it was the latter. But just the same, she unbuttoned her jacket so she could more easily reach her pistol. Was she being paranoid? Probably, she thought. Last she checked, though, paranoia in her line of work wasn't fatal; complacency was.

Unlocking her hotel room, she pushed the door inward and peered inside. Lights were on in the room and from her vantage point it looked in order. She took a step inside, slid the overnight bag's carrying strap from her shoulder and eased the bag to the floor.

Something hard suddenly slammed into her right shoulder blade. The force propelled her body forward, spun her to the left and stole her footing. She tried to correct herself, but landed on her right thigh and ribs. Her elbow caught a lot of the impact and the sharp bolts of pain reverberating through her body caused her to hiss through clenched teeth.

The pale-skinned man who had knocked Young over shut the door behind him.

"Hello, Maxine," he said.

Two men came through the door, brushed past the man who'd just spoken and closed in on Young.

She already had unsheathed her pistol from its holster. She brought the weapon around and punched a 9 mm slug into the forehead of the man closest to her. His head rocked back. Teetering for a stretched second, his limp form suddenly hurtled forward.

Young batted at the onrushing corpse, his eyes locked open, his jaw hanging slack.

By that time, the other two men were on her. While one grabbed her shooting hand, twisting the gun from her grip, she caught a glimpse of the man who'd addressed her by name.

Closing her hand into a fist, she threw a punch that hammered against his jaw. The force of the blow shoved his face to one side. Young's fist had gone numb, but she drew it back for a second strike. A sharp pricking sensation flared in her neck. Both men suddenly stepped away. Her vision blurred almost immediately. Her right hand reached up for the edge of the bed. She willed her fingers to close and grab a handful of the bedspread. They didn't respond.

The face of the man with the waxy skin suddenly appeared inches from her own.

"Good night, Maxine," he said. "Fun's just starting."

His laughter sounded far away as she lost consciousness.

10

"I don't like it," Brognola growled through the phone. "Not one damn bit."

"Join the club," Bolan replied.

The soldier had slipped into one of the bedrooms in the safe house to call Brognola. Sitting in an armchair, he held his cell phone to his ear. He had just told Brognola about his plan to take Davis to the site of the blast that had killed her sister.

"It's crazy," Brognola said. "There's no way you can have her out in the open without putting her at risk. Not to mention the risk to you and the others. I don't mean to sound like a mother hen—"

"We can handle it," Bolan said. "We're going to get in, get out and get on the plane. We'll be back in the States in twenty hours. I promise."

Bolan heard the big Fed make a skeptical noise on the other end of the line.

"I don't like to second guess you, Striker," Brognola said.

"But?"

"But this is reckless. You already accomplished the mission, soldier. It's time to come the hell home."

"I'm not coming home on this one yet," Bolan said.

"For the love of— Okay, why the hell not?"

The Executioner briefed Brognola about Yezhov and the satellites.

"Hell," Brognola said.

"Yeah."

"It's never cut and dry, is it?"

"No…no, it's not. Can you check it out for me?"

"Trust but verify. Always a good strategy. But it's separate from Nightingale—I mean Jennifer Davis, right?"

"How do you mean?"

"You could send her back tonight, right now, and that wouldn't affect your next move on Yezhov."

Bolan closed his eyes, massaged the bridge of his nose with the thumb and forefinger of his right hand.

"I know where you're going with this. And you're wrong."

"You don't identify with her?" Brognola persisted. "Not even a little bit?"

"The revenge thing?"

"Not revenge," Brognola countered. "Justice. When the mob killed your family, you took out the people who caused it. But you kept at it long past the point of revenge. You didn't stop until you gutted them."

"Of course. It was war."

"Right," Brognola said. "Same goes for this lady. If revenge was her motive, she would have quit years ago. That can only sustain a person for so long. She kept fighting, in her own way. I'm no shrink, but I'm guessing Davis didn't just want justice for herself, her twin sister, her family. She wanted others to have it, too."

"To fight for people who couldn't fight for themselves."

"Something like that, yeah. Sound familiar?"

"Mildly," Bolan replied. "You're pretty sharp. Maybe you should get a daytime talk show, interview women who love too much, all that stuff."

Brognola laughed. "And leave this magic behind? Forget it. Look, I trust you, Striker. Just keep your head clear. That's all I am saying. It could go fine. It could go badly. Just watch your ass."

"Understood. You can get me some information on the satellite?"

"I'll have the cyber team dig up what it can and send it to you."

"The delay with Davis coming home, will the White House kick your ass over that?"

"Of course," Brognola replied wearily. "Regardless, just watch your own ass and get home as soon as you can."

BOLAN ALLOWED HIMSELF to drift into a light sleep in the chair. The phone in his lap trilled. His eyes snapped open and he brought the device to his ear.

"Go," he said.

"Striker, it's Barb," Price said.

"Hey," the soldier replied. He shifted in the chair, pressed the palm of his free hand against his right eye, rubbing away any lingering remnants of his nap.

"You were sleeping."

"You know me," Bolan said. "Sleep's a relative term when I am in the field."

"Of course. Hey, I have something for you."

"Great, what is it?"

"I looked into this whole satellite thing," she said. "Our new friend's telling the truth, apparently."

"The satellite program's real."

"Right. And more important, the FBI's counterintelligence people have been tracking one of the scientists, a man named Christopher Rusk, for several months. Guy's been living really well, even for a physicist. He's also made two trips to Moscow in the past three years, ostensibly to speak at scientific conferences in those cities. We have our CIA station chief in Moscow, a guy named Mauldin, combing through his files, checking to see whether he has any information on the guy."

"He under surveillance?"

"Sure," Price said. "FBI tapped his phones and his emails once they opened an investigation into him. We called the special agent in charge. He's got his people scouring the records, but he's not hopeful. Rusk has played it extremely safe. They think he may know he's under suspicion. Emails are clean, same for phone calls. FBI asked if we wanted him rolled up. I said no. You okay with that?"

"Good call," the soldier said. "We may need to jerk his chain later. Especially if we want Yezhov to feel a noose tightening from every direction. For now, just have the Feds shadow him, though."

"Will do. Mauldin, the CIA guy, is also checking into this whole Sindikat thing," Price said. "Or rechecking. Apparently, the CIA and the Defense Intelligence Agency think it's a myth. My NSA contacts aren't so sure."

"Meaning?"

"Meaning they know a lot of the Russian oligarchs are in bed with the bureaucrats. That's old news. Now, whether a select group wants to position itself as a shadow government in Russia or just grab money and power for themselves remains up in the air."

"Not sure I see the difference between the two."

"Well, the NSA folks aren't sure whether it's an organized, concerted effort aimed at controlling the country for the long haul. Or just a loose confederation of crooks hooking up as the need arises."

"If it's the latter, I don't think they'd mess with the directed-energy satellites," Bolan said. "Sure, they might steal the technology, sell or give it to the Russians so they could build one—or a half dozen, for that matter. Beyond that, you're venturing into something much bigger and more organized. This operation has the hallmarks of something bigger, a conspiracy. Keep digging."

"Of course," Price said. "Hal told me you're taking her to the blast site."

"Here we go—" Bolan said.

"Just be careful."

"You know I will."

"I do, but it makes me feel better to say it."

"I'll have her on a plane tomorrow. I'll be back in Virginia sometime after that."

"Make it soon," Price said, before Bolan cut the connection.

WHILE THE SKIES over London remained black, Davis and the others had risen from bed. From his seat in the first-floor dining room, Bolan could hear alarms beep through the floorboards, followed several minutes later by the rush of showers and at least one hair dryer.

Grimaldi was the first to emerge from upstairs. He wore jeans, a charcoal-gray turtleneck and white canvas sneakers. His still-wet hair was combed back from his face.

"You look like shit," Grimaldi said.

"Thanks," Bolan replied. "Feeling even worse."

Several pictures, aerial shots downloaded from the internet, were strewn over the tabletop.

"Aerial shots of the square?"

"Yeah."

"Did you sleep?"

"No," Bolan said.

"You'll be sharp as a knife today."

"Thanks."

"What'd you figure out, looking at the satellite shots?"

Bolan sighed. "There are about a million ways for Yezhov's men to get us. That's if some other freelancer doesn't pop up and try to snatch her first."

"You map out an escape route?"

"Couple of them," Bolan said. "I'll explain them to you when McCarter shows up. Hopefully, we won't have to use them."

"Amen to that."

Grimaldi hoisted his coffee, uncoiled himself from the chair and moved back into the kitchen. Humming, he opened the refrigerator door and scoured its interior for food.

Bolan had considered ordering McCarter, Grimaldi and Ramirez to wait at the airport, but had decided against it. He knew the men, especially McCarter and Grimaldi, and neither needed nor wanted his protection. And, if something happened to Bolan, someone would need to swoop in and make sure Davis made it to the plane and back to the United States.

Once everyone gathered downstairs, Bolan briefed the others on the escape routes.

Grimaldi and McCarter, the two tapped to drive, paid rapt attention. After the briefing, they climbed aboard their vehicles and headed out for the train station.

McCarter drove his Jaguar, while Bolan and Davis rode in the backseat. Grimaldi drove the black Escalade and Ramirez rode shotgun.

Eyes turned toward the rear driver's-side window, Bolan swept his gaze over his surroundings. An M-4 assault rifle fitted with an M-203 grenade launcher stood at an angle in the space between his left leg and the door nearest him. The assault rifle's muzzle poked into the carpeted floor while the retractable stock rested on the seat cushion next to his thigh.

"Do you always travel with this much firepower?" Davis asked.

"At least this much."

"What if we get pulled over?"

"Diplomatic plates. Even with my friend's erratic driving, the police won't bug us."

"At least if I'm driving, the car will make it back to the States," McCarter growled.

"Look," Davis said, "I know you didn't have to do this. All of you guys. Realistically, I'm guessing you could have forced me to go back."

"We left our chloroform-soaked rags at home, or else you'd be on the plane right now," McCarter said while cutting the steering wheel left.

Bolan glanced at the woman, who was opening her mouth to reply, but he beat her to it. "Yes, he's kidding. Yes, we could have forced you to go. Still could, frankly. But I didn't want to go that route."

"Why?"

"This way the U.S. government is recruiting you. The other way is an extraordinary rendition. I've done both. But in my eyes—and Washington's eyes, for that matter—you're not a criminal. If you're a terrorist, you've been terrorizing all the right people."

"That's good to know."

"Second, it's better if you come of your own free will," Bolan said.

"Because?"

"Because otherwise the chances are you'd comply for a while, then say 'screw this,' feel hemmed in and disappear."

"Really? And you know this how?"

Bolan leveled his gaze on her. "I don't. I'm just pulling all this out of my backside."

"He's a keen observer of human nature," McCarter chimed in. "When he's not killing blokes and blowing shit up. Look, we're almost there. Maybe you two can pick up this deep conversation later?"

"THIS IS STUPID," muttered the man seated next to Mikoyan.

Mikoyan plucked the cigar from his mouth, turned and pinned the man under his contemptuous gaze. They were seated inside the cab of a lime-green delivery truck filled with racks of bottled water, the kind used in office water coolers. Fear flickered in the other man's eyes. He licked his lips, fell silent and stared through the truck's windshield.

Satisfied, Mikoyan returned the cigar to his mouth and set his sights back on the train station. The man next to him was beneath contempt, another of Yezhov's foot soldiers, all spit-and-polish, but no guts, no skills. They'd never played a hunch like he was playing. Chances were the woman had gone underground and wouldn't surface for days, weeks, maybe even months. Chances were she was too smart to head to this spot, the train station where her sister was killed, on the anniversary of the bombing.

Chances were...

But Mikoyan knew better than to let that hold him back.

For reasons that escaped him, people became attached to one another, built their lives around each other. When they lost someone, they lost their mind, too. Their judgment. That made them unpredictable, but also weak and easily exploited. Mikoyan had figured that out as a boy growing up in a Russian orphanage. Unlike the other children, he cared little whether he had parents. The attachments just complicated things. And he had little patience for complications.

He thought of the other woman, the former CIA agent, who'd dropped everything to come help her friend. She was still alive for the moment, sleeping off the effects of the drugs she'd been administered. But her drawing breath was a temporary condition. And she was in her current situation because she'd been foolish enough to stick her neck out for another. She would eventually die, at his hands, never knowing her mistake.

A black Jaguar sped past the truck and grabbed his attention. He had just settled his eyes on it, when a second vehicle—a black SUV—rolled by.

"Diplomatic plates," the other man said.

Mikoyan grinned. "Diplomats don't use the subway," he said.

He activated the microphone hooked to the cuff of his left jacket sleeve. Raising his arm, he spoke into it. "They're here," he said.

BOLAN WENT EVA from the Jaguar. He heard a metallic *thunk* and the trunk lid sprang open. He walked around to the rear of the car, reached inside and removed a black leather briefcase. The specially constructed briefcase contained an MP-5. There were two switches built into the handle; one acted as a safety while the second would trigger the weapon. He'd prefer to remove the weapon from the case, but if he found himself with his back against the wall, he could flick the switch and use the spray-and-pray method of gun fighting. He also carried a second Beretta in a dual shoulder rig.

He walked around to Davis's side of the car, eyes scanning the area, and pulled open her door.

"Let's go," he said.

She nodded and climbed from the vehicle. Bolan heard another car door slam. He looked and saw Ramirez had exited the truck and was moving toward them.

The memorial area was empty at this hour. On top of a rectangular plinth stood the statue of an angel, wings spread wide, body covered in a flowing gown. An open hand was pressed over her heart and she cast a pained look skyward. A shallow, circular pool surrounded the plinth and the statue. A pair of smaller pools stood on either side of the larger one, a fountain of water springing up from the center of each.

Bolan saw Davis stare up at the angel, heard her swallow hard. He took a couple of steps back and took another look around at the memorial square. A small building fronted by sliding glass doors and large plate-glass windows stood a dozen or more yards from him. Turnstiles and ticket counters were visible inside the train station's well-lit interior. He guessed the stairs leading to the subway were located farther inside.

A voice buzzed in his radio earpiece.

"Check your six," Grimaldi said. "Possible hostiles. Three of them."

Bolan turned slowly, began backing toward Davis. His thumb rested on the stud that acted as a safety for the encased MP-5. Ramirez apparently heard the same radio traffic, as Bolan noticed he was taking a step forward, sweeping back his jacket and reaching for his pistol.

The soldier spotted three men walking several feet apart from one another in a ragged line across the square. Bolan noticed immediately the man in the middle was unusually tall and pale enough that his face seemed to gleam under the artificial light beaming down from the lampposts. An overcoat hung from the man's narrow shoulders. With his left hand, the man was pressing a mobile phone to his ear. The man's right hand was obscured from view. One of the other men wore a brown leather bomber jacket and jeans. The second was decked out in a blue denim jacket, and had a baseball cap pulled tightly over his head.

The safety off, Bolan rested the ball of his thumb on a second stud that acted as the trigger. By this point, the big American had maneuvered himself between Davis and the three men.

"I'm going EVA," McCarter said through the earphones.

"Negative," Bolan said. "I'm bringing her to the car. Be ready to move. Same for you, Jack."

Bolan grabbed Davis's hand and started to pull her from the memorial.

She turned her face toward him, her expression a mixture of puzzlement and irritation. Her lips parted, a question forming. Bolan shook his head.

"Move," he growled.

Her eyes drifted from Bolan's and over his shoulder. Her eyes widened. Bolan turned in the direction of her gaze. The man in the leather jacket was closing in on them. He raised his hand, which clutched a gun and started to draw down on them.

Squeezing Davis's arm, Bolan triggered the MP-5. A burst fired out through a hole in the side of the briefcase. The Executioner swept the briefcase in a tight circle. Bullets struck the man, lancing through his torso.

As that shooter fell, the soldier's other two opponents, their weapons in view, sprinted in opposite directions. Each laid down fire that flew well over Bolan's head. He guessed they were trying to drive him to ground, but didn't want to chance hurting Davis.

Three more pairs of hardmen, each of them brandishing pistols or submachine guns, converged from different directions.

Autofire chattered behind Bolan. He heard someone cry out behind him. He glanced at Ramirez in time to see the guy collapse to the ground in a boneless heap. Crimson entry wounds, glistening under the artificial light, peppered his back.

"Ramirez! Ramirez!" Bolan shouted into his throat microphone.

The man lay on his stomach, motionless. Blood seeped from beneath his torso, drained into the groove in the bricks covering the ground, forming dozens of rivers of blood.

Bolan had no time to linger on the fallen man. His first duty was to get Davis the hell out of there.

An engine revved to his left and Grimaldi's SUV jumped the curb and carved a path toward Bolan and Davis. It shuddered as it crossed over the uneven terrain of sidewalks and grass. Concrete barriers jutted up from the ground and formed a circle around the monument. Though meant to look like decorations, they actually were meant to prevent the onslaught of a car bomb. Bolan knew he'd have to get Davis outside the barriers before he could shove her into the rear of the armored SUV.

An instant later, another familiar noise rose above the rattling gunfire. The steady thrumming of a helicopter registered with the soldier. He swore under his breath. He doubted the London police already had a bird in the air. And since one of his pilots was possibly dead, and the other was behind the wheel of an idling vehicle, that left only one option.

Yezhov had sent a chopper.

Before he had time to dwell on it, the Executioner caught two men closing in on his right flank. He triggered the MP-5 and laid down a line of fire that chewed into the nearest of the hardmen. The second tried to sprint sideways, squeezing off a quick shot in Bolan's direction.

The bullet whistled past the soldier's ear. He riddled the guy with a punishing burst from the H&K. Letting go of Davis's hand, he drew out the Berettas. The soldier leveled the handguns at another pair of gunners and loosed a rapid succession of tri-bursts from the weapon. The thugs withered under the hail of gunfire.

Pencil-thin lines of flame spat from the twin muzzles of the Berettas as Bolan laid down covering fire and guided Davis toward the SUV. By then, she had produced her .38 revolver. It cracked twice and Bolan saw one of Yezhov's gunners fall. Instead of freezing after killing someone, she was already sweeping her eyes and the pistol's barrel in unison, hunting for another target.

The woman was ready to fight for her life.

Good, Bolan thought.

She had no other choice.

11

McCarter listened to the fighting rage for several seconds, grinding his teeth as he waited on Bolan, Ramirez and Davis to make it back to the memorial. When he heard Ramirez go down, the Phoenix Force commander damn near decided to disobey orders and throw himself into the fray. God knew it wouldn't be the first time he'd saluted an order with his middle finger.

Just then the white glow of headlights appeared behind him, accompanied by the growl of an engine. A red van sped by, tires blazing their way across the pavement toward the memorial. The driver slammed on the brakes and the vehicle screeched to a halt several yards short of the concrete barriers ringing the memorial. The side door of the van slammed open and a man brandishing a shotgun rolled out of the portal. A second man, this one carrying an AK-47, jumped to the ground.

Screw this, McCarter told himself.

He grabbed for the door handle, stopped.

By the time he disembarked from the vehicle and made it to the kill zone, the van would be empty and Bolan would face even greater odds.

Releasing the door handle, he muttered another oath, threw the car into gear and punched the accelerator.

"Sorry, baby," he said to the car.

The car's power pack growled and the vehicle hurtled forward. He cut the wheel left and angled the Jag across the parking lot. As the wheels chewed up asphalt, the vehicle roared ahead and gained speed. Another armed man appeared in the van's side door. He spotted the black sports car bearing down on him and his jaw dropped. The Jag wouldn't gain enough speed to total the van, but it damn sure would damage it.

The car's front end lanced into the side of the van. The impact sent the gunner flying out the side door. He struck the Jaguar's hood, bounced off it and struck the windshield with his head before disappearing over the side of the car. The air bag deployed with a pop, mushrooming from the center of the steering wheel and catching McCarter's face as his head slammed forward.

The car shuddered to a stop. McCarter, his vision still obscured by the bag, felt around for the seat belt buckle. Even as the air bag deflated McCarter unbuckled the seat belt and pushed open the door. He climbed from the vehicle, saw that the front end, once sleek and curvy, was crumpled like a discarded foil sandwich wrapper.

Reaching beneath his jacket, he drew the Brownings, cocked back the hammers.

Moving around the van he spotted the driver's-side door swinging open. A man climbed from inside, a pistol in his hand. The Brownings punched a couple of rounds into the guy's chest and he dropped to the ground.

McCarter moved away from the van. Two more gunners who'd been running toward Bolan halted when the Jag slammed into the van. They turned and headed back to it.

One spotted McCarter and was trying to draw a bead on him with an AK-47. The Browning in McCarter's left hand chugged out two rounds and a pair of crimson geysers sprang from the man's chest. In the same instant, the former SAS fighter snapped off another round with the Browning clutched in his right hand. The shot drilled through the fabric of the man's jacket sleeve before whistling into the darkness. Wielding an Uzi with one hand, the hardman squeezed off a fast burst. The swarm of bullets from the Israeli-made SMG sailed past McCarter's left flank and punched through the front grill and into the engine block of the van parked at his six.

McCarter sighted the Browning on the man's center mass,

tapped out two 9 mm manglers that tore into the man's chest and took him down.

Before he could find another target, thrumming helicopter blades caught the Phoenix Force warrior's ear. He looked skyward and spotted a chopper buzzing over a line of buildings fixed across the street from the memorial.

He guessed it wasn't one of theirs. Bloody wonderful, he thought.

BOLAN TUGGED Davis's arm and jerked his head toward the cars.

"C'mon!" he shouted.

Davis nodded her understanding. Bolan, taking hold of her hand, surged toward the parking lot. The ring of concrete barriers lay a couple dozen yards away.

Within moments, the helicopter glided into position, like a black shark swimming overhead. The roar of the engines swallowed up the yelling from Yezhov's men, drowned out the popping of gunfire.

Bolan saw muzzle-flashes erupt from next to the SUV and stab into the dark sky. Bullets struck the bottom of the helicopter, sparked against its steel skin and ricocheted into the darkness.

A flash of motion in the corner of Bolan's eye caused him to turn. He caught a pair of shooters, one armed with an Uzi, the other with a Mossberg pump shotgun, closing in. The Beretta in the big American's left hand churned out a series of three-round bursts as he made a horizontal sweep with the weapon. Even as they collapsed to the ground, Bolan heard Davis gasp. Whipping his head around, he followed her gaze and saw a shooter marching toward them, bringing his Steyr AUG to bear on Bolan. Before the guy could line up a shot, though, Bolan triggered the Beretta again. One round punched through the man's cheek, while a second drilled into his right eye socket.

Before another heartbeat could pass, Bolan felt something hammer into his side like a cannonball. The impact caused him to belch air from his lungs and thrust him to the ground. His attacker, a rangy man with mouse-brown hair, came to rest on top of Bolan and drew back his fist, preparing to pound Bolan in the face.

But the man suddenly froze. His upper torso jerked, heralding the bullets that tore through the man's chest, exploding outward with geysers of blood. By this time, the whirring of the chopper blades had grown loud enough that Bolan couldn't hear the burst of autofire that felled his attacker. The man teetered for a moment before Bolan shoved him aside. He rolled onto all fours then sprang to his feet.

He fisted his remaining Beretta. Leveling the weapon at shoulder height, Bolan swept its muzzle over the area, hunting for another target while also looking for Davis.

Just then Bolan saw that the helicopter had descended, hovering just a few feet from the ground. The side door gaped open, and two men were dragging Davis toward the craft, one holding on to each arm. Bolan, already surging toward the helicopter, watched Davis struggling against her captors' grip.

One of Yezhov's men, armed with an assault rifle, stepped into view in the helicopter's door. The man's weapon flared to life. Slugs hammered into the ground a couple of feet from Bolan and sent plumes of brick dust bursting upward. The soldier bolted to the right, then cut left, carving out a zigzag pattern to make himself a harder target.

The men who'd grabbed Davis shoved her into the helicopter's interior and climbed in behind her. The roar of its engines intensified and the craft climbed skyward.

When Davis disappeared from view, Bolan drew a bead on the gunman who'd been showering him with lead. The triple-round volleys from the Beretta lanced into the man's chest and throat. The assault rifle slipped from dead fingers, fell to the ground. The corpse swayed on his feet for a stretched second before he pitched forward, falling from the helicopter.

The soldier stood and watched as the craft ascended. An unfamiliar feeling of helplessness washed over him as the helicopter—and Davis—moved farther from reach. It stopped for an instant, hovered. Bolan tensed, waiting for its occupants to open fire again. With precise, quick movements, he ejected a spent magazine from the Beretta, fed another into its grip. Even as his hands worked the 93-R's slide, he watched as the helicopter lurched forward, carving a path into the horizon.

THE EXECUTIONER clamped his jaw shut until it ached and surveyed the carnage around him.

He counted thirteen dead, including Ramirez. The first seam of the orange-red dawn broke through the night sky. But the overhead lights continued to shower the place with a whitish cast that made the faces of the corpses littering the ground around him glow, their pooled blood glisten.

Nice play, soldier. You lost Jennifer Davis. The mistake very likely would cost the young hacker her life. That loss also could harm the country's security. And Ramirez, who was a hell of a good soldier, was dead.

He had sent the Farm a text message, giving them the barest outline, then stowed the telephone. Police cruisers already were roaring into the parking lot and Bolan guessed he was going to spend the night in a police station, trying to explain what in the hell had transpired.

Bolan sensed someone coming up from behind. Turning, he saw Grimaldi approaching, a grim expression on the pilot's face.

"You okay, Sarge?"

Bolan shook his head.

"We'll find her," Grimaldi said. "We'll get her back."

Before Bolan could reply, he heard car doors slamming and police barking orders.

Grimaldi flashed what Bolan could tell was a halfhearted grin.

"Time to assume the position, I guess," the pilot said, slowly bringing up his hands. "If you have an escape plan, I'm all ears."

Bolan raised his hands, too.

12

Russia

Yezhov never had expected to return.

He stood on the driveway—a fissured ribbon of concrete, waist-high weeds jutting through the crack—and stared at the main resort building. Exposure to the elements and time had bleached the exterior paint, caused it to bubble and peel.

The hundred-acre resort had sprung up a few years after the Soviet Union had fallen. A group of Western investors had invaded the country, their pockets stuffed with dollars, heads equally swollen with ideas of how they'd stake a claim in the wild frontiers of Russia after they'd already put a stake through the heart of the Russian bear.

The investors had outfitted the property with two paved airstrips and a helipad to make the place accessible to cargo planes and those well-heeled enough to charter flights to the remote location. The plan had been for the place to cater to rich men who wanted to hunt bears and other wildlife, while their wives wiled away their time by the indoor pool, on a massage table or in the salon. Most of the customers were high-level executives, self-proclaimed masters of the universe, looking to dominate their surroundings. The chance to embark on the Russian equivalent of a safari in snow-capped mountains had proven an irresistible call for many, at least at first. From what Yezhov heard later, most of the hunters were morons, a bigger danger to themselves than to the surrounding wildlife. Trust-fund babies and CEOs who equated their talent and lust for hardball negotiations carried out in air-conditioned conference rooms, while decked out in three-hundred-dollar shirts, hair coifed to standards usually reserved for Hollywood starlets, with animal toughness.

Yezhov drew deep from his cigarette, held the smoke in his lungs for a couple of seconds before expelling twin tendrils of it through flared nostrils. He took another drag. More than one of these men—allegedly the top of the food chains—would panic at the sight of a charging bear. The ones who didn't scream and piss themselves, sometimes managed to squeeze off a shot. They'd wing the animal, forcing the guides, men who'd hunted the mountains since boyhood, to deliver a kill shot to the animal. One such man had delivered the death blow to the resort. When this particular group had come upon a pair of cubs, they'd decided to wait for the mother to return. She did and, smelling man, flew into a rage. True to form, the internet executive had grazed the charging mother bear in the back leg, sent her into a roll. Fueled by adrenaline and idiocy, he'd broken ranks, charged the wounded animal, apparently planning a close-range kill.

Within a heartbeat, the bear sprang on the man. Claws and teeth rent flesh, stained and spotted the snow with crimson. By the time the guides had downed the bear, the executive lay in the snow, brand-new hunting togs slashed, flesh flayed. Unbidden, a smile ghosted the Yezhov's lips. They hadn't realized that a bear was most dangerous when it was cornered.

Within a year, business plummeted. The stream of high rollers wanting to test themselves against nature, cement their place at the top of the food chain, dwindled to a trickle.

The wind picked its pace, wildly whipped the tails of his coat around his ankles. The cold bit into the skin of the Russian's face and hands. Yezhov had been only too happy to buy the place for next to nothing. He cared little for the hospitality industry and the business was a dog. But it allowed him yet another vessel to launder cash. When it'd become too much of a pain, he'd shuttered the place. Ninety percent had gone to seed with his blessing. However, years of experience told him conditions could change in a heartbeat. When they did, it helped to have a place to go. He'd stockpiled the place full of weapons, had reinforced the ground-level doors, barred the windows, secured the rooftops. A network of security cameras dotted the landscape. The fleet garage contained a half-dozen armored Humvees and two similarly equipped Mercedes sedans. The lower level included well-maintained living quarters and a command center capable of monitoring the various cameras, sensors and alarms on the property.

A dozen or so of his best men already had traveled to back him up. At least another dozen was on its way, lured by promises of big paydays. If this Matt Cooper made it to the grounds— *if*—he'd not cover more than a few yards before Yezhov's crews cut him down.

Yezhov had planned for everything.

HER EYES OPENED.

Smears of light and the sensation of her back pressed against the cold, hard floor greeted Jennifer Davis as awareness seeped back in, breaking up the darkness.

She squinted against the glare. Her attention turned inward to the relentless throb rocking her temples, the heaviness in her arms and legs. Allowing her head to loll to one side, she pressed her cheek to the floor. The cold from the floor tiles soothed her pounding head. For a moment, she thought the darkness might pull her under again.

With a sharp intake of air, her eyes popped open and her heartbeat accelerated. Memories returned, first a trickle, but quickly a rushing torrent. The hotel. A forearm, corded with muscle, looped around her neck, stopped her in her tracks. Another hand clamped over her mouth before she could scream. A sharp prick in the neck, followed by darkness.

And presently she was awake here. Just where the hell was she? Her eyes had finally adjusted to the light and she surveyed her surroundings, which told her nothing. A square room, lined with painted concrete brick walls, sealed with a heavy door of some blond-colored wood. Her gaze settled for a moment on where the doorknob and dead-bolt lock should have been. Both were missing, the spots where they should have been were covered by smooth steel discs secured by screws. She saw no obvious cameras, but that didn't mean none were in the room.

Fear caused her heartbeat to speed up again. This time, the sudden rush of adrenaline cut through the lingering effects of the sedative. She sat up. Unconsciously, her hands balled up into fists. Great, she thought, I'm locked in a plain-vanilla broom closet. Somewhere in the world. Was she still in Moscow or somewhere else? She had no way of even knowing at this point.

The anger quickly turned to fear. Matt Cooper's words came back to her. The memory caused a cold tickle of fear to race down her spine. If someone caught her, he'd explained, they'd work her over, use every lever possible against her. She'd already proved just by the path she'd chosen that people mattered over all else, that she'd surrender a normal life and happiness for revenge. That she was willing to put her sister—or her sister's memor—above all else. The people she'd been dealing with knew that. They'd know they could use the safety of other members of her family, her friends from her former life, people from her network, to pressure her into doing as they ordered. They'd probe her mind, every last memory of the last several years, to grab every last dime she'd taken. Anyone she'd given money to would end up a target.

A heavy sensation she recognized as guilt settled over her. All these people, she'd put them at risk just to sate her own thirst for revenge. Some of them, the ones who'd worked alongside her during the past few years, had believed in her, had trusted her. An awful realization that she'd failed them, hell, had put them in danger just by associating with her, dawned on her. The guilt dissipated, replaced by a squeezing sensation in her heart, an ache in her throat. Tears stung the corners of her eyes.

She clamped them shut. The memory of another face came to her. Her face, but not her face. Though they'd been twins, Jessica's features always had differed slightly, especially as they'd aged. Her cheekbones were sharper, her lips fuller. A smoother forehead, the slight upturn at the corners of her lips, reflected her more carefree attitude. Would Jessica have wanted this for her twin sister? Living as a fugitive, using false identities, separated from family and friends?

Davis had entertained this question before, albeit briefly. Deep down, she knew the answer, hated it, ran from it. No, her sister wouldn't have wanted this for her. Just like Davis knew she'd never wish her life on anyone else. The people she'd allied herself with through the years knew the risks, made their own decisions. But even so, she'd only let any of them become involved as much as necessary, shared only as much as they needed to know. The rest, she'd kept to herself or shared with Maxine Young or, to a lesser extent, Nigel Lawson.

No, clearly, Jessica would never have wanted any of this for her twin sister, Davis had told herself more than once. She'd imagined them living a few blocks apart from one another in some suburb with perfect houses, husbands, kids and dogs. Hell, on the rare instance when Davis allowed herself to think about it, she admitted that she'd wanted that, too.

Unconsciously, she drew her knees up toward her chest, looped her arms around them to hold them there. She looked around at the bland walls that surrounded her, the door with no knob, and realized just how trapped she really was. Pull it together, girl, she admonished herself. This may not be what you wanted, but it's what you have. You can sit here, wait on them to probe your mind like a science experiment, probably inject you full of more drugs, torture you. Or you can do something.

Sure, she told herself. But do what?

13

"Cooper?"

Bolan nodded. The CIA guy flashed Bolan a big toothy grin, swung open the door and gestured for him to enter. A brass nameplate on the door identified the office's occupant as Charlie Parker, which Bolan knew was an alias.

The Executioner entered the office while the man closed the door behind him. Bolan guessed the agent to be a few inches less than six feet. The top of his head was an exposed dome of shiny pink skin, blemished by an occasional freckle. The gray hair that remained on the sides and rear of his skull had been shorn close to the skin. His khaki pants were neatly pressed as was his blue-and-white striped dress shirt. His black wingtip shoes gleamed like the skin of his exposed scalp.

The man extended a hand and Bolan took it.

"Mauldin," the other man said as they shook hands.

"That your first or last name?" Bolan asked.

"Yes," Mauldin said. He gestured toward a pair of leather armchairs separated by a circular coffee table. "Have a seat."

Bolan took the hint, left the question at the door and lowered himself into the nearest chair.

Movement to Bolan's left registered in his peripheral vision. He turned and saw a large gray bird walking sideways across the carpet, bobbing its head.

"It's an African gray parrot," Mauldin said. "Name's Charlie Jr.—I bring him to work every day. Don't worry, he won't hurt you."

"I'm relieved."

Grinning, Mauldin knelt down. He held out his hand, fingers extended, but pressed together. He held the hand sideways, the index finger jutting forward, the other three fingers curled. The bird bobbed its head once again, then raised a talon, clamped it around Mauldin's index finger and did the same with his other talon.

Mauldin returned to standing, eyes fixed on the bird.

"C'mon, you big 'fraidy cat," he said. He carried the bird to a large square cage that stood in the corner. He slipped it inside the cage, and it disembarked from his finger onto a wooden rod that ran across the length of the cage. Shutting the cage door, Mauldin turned toward Bolan.

"He's scared of you," he said. "Nothing personal—he's scared of everyone."

Bolan nodded.

"You got the Beretta?" Mauldin asked.

The soldier pulled aside the left edge of his black leather bomber jacket, exposed the Beretta 93-R he carried in a shoulder rig. It had been waiting for him in his hotel room when he'd arrived.

"Stupendous," Mauldin said. "You checked it, didn't you? Doesn't happen often, but occasionally housekeeping finds a package like that, it disappears. They sell it for a few rubles. Good for them, bad for me. Right? Once in a while, one of them actually has a conscience. They take it to the police...who turn around and sell it on the black market."

"Who can you trust?" Bolan asked rhetorically.

"That's all I'm saying," Mauldin replied. He set a cup of coffee on the table in front of Bolan. "You take it black, right? You look like a guy who takes his coffee black."

The soldier picked up the cup and sipped. The coffee was good.

Bolan swept his gaze over the room. In some ways, it was unremarkable. A large desk, the wood stained a deep amber color, stood a few feet from the back wall, which was lined with bookshelves. A couple of abstract paintings that reminded Bolan of dog vomit were posted on two of the walls. However, a large poster of Charlie Parker, the jazz musician, framed and behind glass, hung on another wall. There also were a half-dozen paintings of birds—a flock of geese, a bald eagle, etc.—moored to the walls.

"Like the bird motif?" Mauldin asked. "Figure if I'm going to use Charlie Parker as an alias, I may as well take it all the way. So I am a jazz fan with the good fortune to be named for a jazz great. And I'm so caught up in it, I have to surround myself with birds, too."

He noticed there were no windows.

"Place is locked down as tight as the proverbial drum," Mauldin said, as though reading Bolan's thoughts. "No windows. Secure doors, phones, computer systems. Completely soundproof. Three guys from the embassy come over and sweep the place twice a day for bugs. They use three because, maybe the Russians will turn one, possibly two, but never all three. You couldn't be safer if you were in your mommy's womb."

"Good to know," Bolan said. "What did Langley tell you?"

"I'm supposed to help," Mauldin said. "Give you weapons, intel, the usual."

"They tell you why?"

Mauldin shrugged. "They told me it involves Yezhov. I know him. He's a prick. He's torched more than one of my assets in his day. Bring me his head and I'll use it for a doorstop."

"I'll keep that in mind," Bolan said.

"Do that. This other thing? About the Sindikat? Sorry, chief, but I think *that* is a bullshit sandwich. I've been here for a decade. We've got Russian mob. We've got crooked politicians. We've got Islamic terrorists. I don't know anything about the Sindikat."

"Never heard rumors?"

"Sure, I've heard rumors. I've heard rumors Joseph Stalin was an alien, sent to take over the world. I've heard rumors they keep Adolf Hitler's brain alive in a jar somewhere, use mediums to talk to it. Never found an alien. Never talked to Hitler's brain. I tend to deal in facts."

Nodding, Bolan leaned forward and set his mug on the table.

"The Sindikat exists," the warrior said. "Trust me on that."

"Fair enough," Mauldin said. "I'm not saying it doesn't. But I have no real information telling me it does. Believe what you want. If you're out to prove they exist, I have no intelligence that can help. That's what I'm saying."

"Understood," Bolan said.

"Good. What I can do is point you to some people who do know. Unfortunately, they won't be happy to see you. They'll likely put up a hell of a fight. Nothing a strapping young man such as yourself can't handle. And I can provide you with more weapons."

Mauldin drew a quick sip from his mug, set it down and gave a satisfied sigh. He held up his right hand, index finger extended skyward. "That reminds me," he said. "I have something for you."

He rose from his chair, made a beeline for his desk and walked around behind it. Bolan watched as he opened a drawer. Even though he thought he knew what the guy was doing, the soldier immediately tensed and, without thinking, looked harder at the agent. The Executioner moved in a world of shadows populated by betrayal. He had no reason to distrust Mauldin, but no reason to trust him, either. He was neutral on whether this man was neutral.

The CIA man drew out a rectangular box that, from a distance, looked as though it was made of black plastic or some composite material. With his other hand, he drew out a cloth sack, the fabric pulled taut by the weight of its contents. He returned and handed the box to Bolan, who took it. The soldier set it on his lap, unsnapped the latches and popped the top open. A .44-caliber Desert Eagle was inside the case.

"Nice gun," Mauldin said. He'd returned to his seat, legs crossed, and he was torching the tip of a cigar with the flame from a stainless-steel lighter. "Hope you don't mind. I took it out, fired a box of shells through it. The guy I buy weapons from, he always gives me Grade A stuff. I trust him. It doesn't hurt to trust, but always verify."

He nodded toward the cloth bag that lay at Bolan's feet. "Extra clips and a holster."

Bolan nodded his thanks. He fed a magazine into the butt of the Desert Eagle, chambered a round and set the safety. Reaching inside the bag, he drew out the holster, clipped it onto his belt at the small of his back.

"I'll need more guns. And other things, too."

"Give me a list," the man said, dragging from his cigar.

"Right." Bolan holstered the Desert Eagle. He settled back into the chair with his coffee.

"Langley told me almost nothing. But they said these pukes have a hostage."

Bolan nodded. "Yes, a woman."

"This a personal thing."

"Meaning?"

"She a girlfriend, a fiancée? A wife? You don't have a wedding ring, but that doesn't mean anything. Not necessarily. I know married guys who don't wear wedding rings. Some don't want to call attention to it, don't want to put their families at risk. Others are just tomcats. She a side dish to your heaping helping of married life?"

"You talk a lot," Bolan responded.

"My style."

"Engaging."

"Look, you seem really intense. Maybe you're always that way. You don't strike me as a funny-nose-and-glasses guy. I get it. Just thought you might have some kind of personal stake in it."

Bolan nodded.

"I do. I told her she'd be safe with me. She wasn't. That's unacceptable," Bolan said.

"A damsel in distress."

The soldier shook his head. "She's not helpless. But she needs help. Besides, I made a promise."

"There's also the national security thing."

"Yeah."

"That's a secondary consideration," Mauldin said, posing it more as a statement than a question.

Bolan shifted uncomfortably in his chair. He was used to

asking questions, not fielding them. Still, he thought about what Mauldin was asking.

"Try coequal considerations," he said after several seconds. "I swore to protect my country. Letting something happen to it would be unacceptable. Letting something happen to her would be unacceptable. And, in this case, it would put the country at risk, too."

"Fair enough," Mauldin said. "Okay, after Langley called, I cast out my lines. Let's reel a couple in and see what we find."

THE FIRST FEW CALLS had yielded nothing. Bolan was now drinking his second cup of coffee while Mauldin worked the phones. The soldier began to feel restless. In sniper or surveillance scenarios, he could sit for hours, moving only as much as necessary. He could forgo sleep, food and water for hours. Sitting still didn't bother him, but sitting still while someone else took action did.

Mauldin killed the connection on his phone, slammed it down on the desktop.

"Damn!" the CIA man muttered.

"Nothing?" Bolan asked.

"Nothing."

"You sure talked a lot for nothing. You were on the horn, what, thirty minutes?"

Mauldin leaned back in his swivel chair, pressed his palms against his eyes and let out a frustrated groan. "Damn, damn, damn."

Suddenly, he pulled his hands away from his eyes, a grin playing on his lips. "Got it," he said.

Mauldin picked up the phone, punched in a series of numbers, pressed it against his ear and listened to it ring. He glanced at Bolan and covered the mouthpiece with his hand. "Freelance pilot. One of Moscow's best."

Bolan nodded.

"Alexi? It's Charlie Parker. Yeah, the bird guy," Mauldin said, using his alias. "Life good? Good. My life? Shit sandwich without the bread, my friend." Mauldin, laughing heartily at his own joke, leaned forward and retrieved a fresh cigar from a hand-carved box sitting on his desk. The CIA agent, the phone squeezed between his ear and his shoulder, slipped the cigar's tip into a single-bladed guillotine and trimmed it. He lit the cigar with his stainless-steel lighter, but continued talking.

"Yeah, I said Yezhov," Mauldin snapped. "What are you deaf? So, you doing any work for him? What's that? You don't know him? Two minutes ago, you knew him. What the hell changed in the last one hundred and twenty seconds? You get amnesia?"

Mauldin fell silent and Bolan could hear the man on the other end of the line speaking rapidly.

"Oh, I see. You don't want to piss him off. Look, I won't tell him where I heard any of this." More rapid speaking on the other end of the line. "You feel uncomfortable telling me this? Really? Okay, listen, Alexi, I didn't want to play this card, but you leave me no choice. Let's talk about the pictures. Hey, don't scream at me. You're the one who got drunk and hooked up with a prostitute. That's on you. I just happened to get pictures of the whole thing. You're not exactly a prize to look at."

With his free hand, Mauldin pulled the cigar from his mouth and blew smoke rings at the ceiling. He let Alexi rant for a couple of minutes before he cut him off.

"You feel better? No? Tough. I'm not your damn therapist. Hey, tell me something, anything, about Yezhov. I'll go the hell away. Promise. My word is my bond."

Mauldin held up his left hand so Bolan could see the first two fingers were crossed.

Mauldin said, "Okay, now you're talking, Alexi." He pulled the cigar from his mouth and set it, smoke curling up from the tip, in a clear-glass ashtray. Picking up a disposable blue ballpoint pen, he scrawled some notes on a small memo pad. After a few minutes of talking, he thanked Alexi for the information, said goodbye and hung up the phone.

"What did he say?" Bolan said.

Mauldin retrieved the cigar from the ashtray, dragged on it for a couple of seconds and returned it to the ashtray.

"My source said some of Yezhov's people were sniffing around for people to make last-minute flights for him."

"I thought Yezhov had plenty of planes."

"Apparently not," Mauldin said, shrugging.

"Maybe. What was the destination?"

"Alexi didn't know."

"Didn't know or didn't want to say?"

Mauldin smirked. "Listen, if you'd ever met Alexi's wife, you wouldn't ask. Seriously, she's small, but she's got an acid tongue that could burn through battleship steel. Even worse, she has three brothers each bigger and crazier than the last. If she saw the photos I have, Alexi would be begging to live in a gulag, I kid you not."

The CIA man paused. He leaned forward and, forearms resting on the desktop, interlaced his fingers. Bolan noticed the guy was staring right at his face, scrutinizing him for some clue about what the Executioner was thinking.

"You don't believe me," Mauldin said.

"I believe you believe what you're saying," Bolan replied. "But that doesn't make it true."

"Look, I know I act like a buffoon," Mauldin said, his voice lowering in volume and slowing in tempo. "I'm not an idiot. I've been running operations in Moscow for years. Before that, I ran them in Beirut and Riyadh. I could tell you chapter and verse everything happening in the Saudi ruling family. Who was getting a little ass on the side. Who lost his monthly stipend gambling in Las Vegas. Who had an addiction to internet porn. I know when an asset's shining me. I know when the other team's using a dangle operation to throw me off track. Alexi's not doing that."

"You believe that?"

Mauldin nodded. "Bet your ass I do. He's not an honorable guy. He's not a nice guy. But he is someone focused on self-preservation. If I drop those pictures in the mail, he'll end up floating facedown somewhere. His brothers-in-law are small-time hoods, but they're connected enough that they could kill Alexi and never have the police say 'boo' about it. Of that, I am certain."

"Okay, assuming Yezhov needed pilots and planes, what did he need them for?"

"Supply run," Mauldin replied. "Ferry food, vehicles and gear.

Yeah, *that* kind of gear. Alexi told me the guy who approached him about it mentioned that they'd be carrying guns and ammunition."

"And take it where?"

Mauldin shrugged. "That's the million-dollar question, isn't it? Unfortunately, Alexi doesn't know. They had a special protocol for it. You agree to do it, they tell you the destination, not the other way around."

Impatience gnawed at Bolan. He wanted to be moving, not jawboning.

"Who does know?"

"Yeah, that's where it gets a little more interesting—and dangerous," Mauldin said. "When he turned it down, Alexi suggested someone else for the job, someone who's going to complicate the hell out of things."

"Explain."

"Does the name Shota Chernkova ring a bell?"

Bolan pondered it for a few seconds. "Negative."

"Man, you need to get to this side of the world more. Anyway, Chernkova is what we call a logistics specialist." Mauldin formed air quotes around "logistics specialist" as he spoke. "He has a small fleet of airplanes and he runs all kinds of contraband around the world. Ships weapons for a lot of the intelligence agencies."

"Including ours?"

"Need-to-know basis, my friend," Mauldin said, grinning. "Problem with him, he's a little bit of a psychopath. Actually, a lot of a psychopath. Not quite Yezhov quality, but pretty damn close."

"We all fall short somewhere," Bolan said.

"Crap, was that a joke? Did you just make a funny? Must be the caffeine. Difference between him and Yezhov is he has a paranoia that outweighs his importance. Back when the Cold War ended, he bought a small airbase outside Moscow. It's pretty tiny by military standards. Mostly was an aircraft-maintenance facility. Perfect for him, though. It had hangars and a couple of runways. Just what he needs for his smuggling operation. Runs a tight ship, too. The French, the Israelis, the British, all have tried to insert people in there. Failed miserably. Most of their guys ended up dead."

"You have any assets inside?"

Mauldin grinned again, held up his right hand, first two fingers forming a V. "Two," he said. "One's a pilot, the other's a mechanic. First guy's a dick and he has a massive gambling problem. That means he owes lots of money to people, none of whom like him. The mechanic, I used an old-fashioned honey trap to catch him. He never saw it coming, if you'll pardon the expression."

"Pardoned."

"He's actually a decent guy. Family man who made a one-time mistake. I'd almost feel bad if he wasn't helping to run guns to al Qaeda and Hezbollah. But he's the maintenance manager. He sees all the paperwork for the flights."

"Perfect, call him," Bolan said.

Mauldin held up his hand, palm facing forward, in a halt gesture. "Here's the problem. Chernkova runs the place like an armed camp. He keeps his people there sometimes for weeks at a time, limits their contact with the rest of the world. His people monitor staff phone calls, emails, family visits, the whole nine yards. It's like a counterintelligence program on steroids. Crazy shit."

"When does the mechanic get a pass?"

"Three days. We were supposed to meet in three days. We'll have to wait."

Bolan shook his head. "I don't have that kind of time," he said. "I need another plan."

"Such as?"

"I'm going in."

"Did you not hear me? The place is an armed camp," Mauldin said.

"Then I guess I'll need more intel and more guns."

MAULDIN SPENT THE NEXT four hours gathering both the information and gear that Bolan would require.

In the meantime, Bolan sent an armored SUV to pick up Mc-

Carter and Grimaldi from the U.S. embassy and bring them to Mauldin's office.

When they arrived, Mauldin had broken away from his telephone and computer long enough to step out and grab carry-out food from an American burger chain located down the street. A copier/printer stood in the corner, making a humming noise as it spit out pages.

McCarter bulled his way through the door. Bolan watched as his comrade halted and took the place in. The Phoenix Force commander paused over the caged bird and did the same with the pictures and statues of birds. While he gave the place a once-over, Grimaldi made a beeline for the coffeemaker.

"Looks like a damn animal preserve," the Briton groused. "Where's my safari hat?"

"I thought you Brits were polite," Bolan said. "Grab a cup of coffee and sit."

"Just making an observation," McCarter said.

"Helpful," Bolan replied.

Ten minutes later, Mauldin returned and Bolan made vague introductions, using only McCarter's and Grimaldi's first names. As the Stony Man warriors downed food and coffee, Mauldin went to work. He grabbed an inch-thick stack of papers from the printer's output tray, separated it into three piles and passed out the packets to his guests. He powered up his laptop computer and, while he waited, lowered a screen from the ceiling. An image of the PC's desktop flashed on the screen

"I brought them up to speed on Chernkova," the Executioner said.

"And your bird fetish," Grimaldi added.

"I prefer fixation," Mauldin said. "Less of the 'ick' factor."

Bolan held up his copy of Mauldin's report. "Brief us on this," he said, getting to the matter at hand.

"Okay, just one second," Mauldin said. He maneuvered the arrow-shaped cursor onto a file name, clicked twice on it. A moment later an overhead shot of a large chunk of property filled the screen. From what he saw, Bolan guessed photo analysts already had pored over it. The property's borders already had been highlighted with a thick white line. Estimated measurements in kilometers and yards were superimposed on the image, arrows pointed to buildings, identifying them as the control tower, the administrative headquarters, barracks, etc.

"All right, ladies, here's the broad brush. This image came from a commercial satellite-imagery firm. But the intel's good. Langley's greatest minds pored over it, then sent it back to me. I vetted the information with my people inside Chernkova's facility, who confirmed most everything here."

Bolan nodded.

"At any given time," Mauldin continued, "Chernkova has between forty-five and fifty gunners on the property. An eclectic mix of mercenaries, soldiers and security pros. Most are exiled from their home countries, and a couple are the targets of arrest warrants from the Hague. Some are high-ranking rejects from the Egyptian, Libyan, Iraqi and Balkan militaries, as well as from some of Africa's worst hellholes—Liberia, Sierra Leone, Somalia. When their strongman governments got busted down, poor bastards needed a place to go. Chernkova was happy to take them in."

"The kind-hearted patriarch," McCarter muttered.

"You will likely find about a dozen, maybe fifteen guys working at any one time. He runs them three shifts. That means you'll catch some guys in the rack, some watching television, eating, torturing small animals. Whatever these creeps do in their spare time. That means you'll surprise about two thirds of them. That's the upside. Downside is, you'll likely encounter more than one wave as they pull their heads from their asses. You don't need me to school you in tactics, but I'd humbly suggest you hit fast and hit hard."

"That's the plan," Bolan said.

14

The airfield seemed to rise out of nowhere, a cluster of concrete and steel in the middle of barren land covered with scrub brush, dirt and rock. During the Cold War, the sprawling facility had served as a place to fix Soviet fighter jets and military cargo planes. That period may be over, but the airfield still buzzed with activity. Antonov An-22 and Ilyushin IL-76 air freighters stood on the tarmac. Engines rumbled as the planes idled. The heat they gave off caused the air above the waiting planes to shimmer. Men and women dressed in midnight blue, insulated jumpsuits scurried around, loading planes, inspecting landing gear, watching as the planes refueled.

Chernkova stood outside the squat, four-story building that housed his offices and watched the activity. A hand-rolled cigarette pinched between his lips burned, emitting a curl of gray smoke. Stiff winds whipped over the wide expanses of open land, tousling his thinning gray hair and sending the cigarette smoke back into his eyes. The sting from the smoke caused him to squint involuntarily.

A lanky man given to wearing blue jeans and casual shirts, Chernkova hardly looked like a millionaire, though he was several times over. His expression remained flat, impenetrable. Small, pale blue eyes took in everything, reacted to nothing. His emotional landscape was as barren as the one surrounding the airport, gray and featureless, save for occasional bouts of rage sparked by primal instincts for self-preservation.

Kimber Twin pistols were sheathed in a custom shoulder rig

wrapped around his slender torso and covered by a brown leather bomber jacket. The guns were a gift from a commander with Pakistani intelligence—a token of appreciation after Chernkova had made an eleventh-hour delivery of assault rifles, body armor and Semtex explosives to Lashkar-e-Taiba. He cared little about the commander's gratitude, but he liked the guns and wore them whenever on the grounds. It telegraphed to his people that he was in charge, a man willing to go to war to protect what was his.

"Sir?" The husky male voice came from behind. Chernkova spun around. A guard stood there, waiting. The man, togged in camouflage fatigues and a field jacket, stared down at Chernkova with dead eyes.

"What?"

"We need to get you inside," the guard said.

A cold finger of fear traced the length of Chernkova's spine. "What is it, what's going on?"

"We have an unidentified chopper coming this way. It was flying too low for our radars to catch. One of our spotters caught a visual of it. We have no scheduled arrivals."

"You're certain it's coming here."

The man glanced left, then right at the open spaces that surrounded them. "Not much else out here, is there, sir?"

Chernkova nodded, then asked, "Just one?"

"Just one."

"ETA?"

"Maybe five minutes. We need to get you inside."

By then, two more guards had appeared and positioned themselves on either side of Chernkova. He stared at the sky, saw nothing but steel-gray clouds overhead and a jagged line of mountains in the distance. It was a reflexive movement. But logic reminded him that, if the helicopter was several minutes away, catching it with the naked eye would be impossible. Doubt crept in for a moment. Was there really a helicopter? Was this a mistake? Were his own people testing him, wanting to see whether he would panic? Perhaps the motives were more sinister, an attempt to take him down, take what he had. He believed the term was "palace coup." He looked at the guards, studied each of their stony visages, which betrayed nothing.

With another glance at the sky, the moment of hesitation passed, swallowed up by Chernkova's desire for self-preservation.

"Let's go," he said. "Have you put the other shifts on alert?"

"Already done. We're trying to hail the chopper. If they don't respond, we'll take them out of the sky with shoulder-fired rockets," the guard said.

Chernkova nodded and started back for the door of his administrative headquarters. The basement of the drab building contained a small command center complete with a sealed room filled with provisions and weapons. If it came to a standoff, he was well prepared.

And, in order for there to be a standoff, the intruders would have to penetrate a wall of more than two dozen well-armed, well-trained guards—a virtual impossibility.

McCARTER FLUNG OPEN the helicopter's side door before the craft reached Chernkova's stronghold. The rotor wash from the main propeller whipped through the door, rippling the fabric of his black fatigues. Two fast ropes were coiled on the floor of the helicopter in front of the door, and Bolan was busy securing these hooked end of the ropes to steel loops built into the chooper's floor. Giving the second rope a final tug, he judged it was secure. He looked up at McCarter and flashed the man a thumbs-up. McCarter acknowledged him with a nod.

The soldier was togged in his black combat suit. The Desert Eagle rode in a thigh holster while the Beretta was snug in a shoulder holster. A Heckler & Koch MP-7 hung from a strap looped over his left shoulder. The assault weapon's stock rested against the shoulder's blade, while the muzzle pointed at the floor. A 40-round clip jutted from the sound-suppressed weapon's grip. Grenades and a combat knife were clipped to his web gear, along with extra magazines for both the H&K and the two handguns. He carried garrotes, bandages, compresses and other gear in the pockets of his pants.

Bolan glanced up at McCarter, who was slipping on gloves to

protect his hands during the slide down the rope. Bolan knew the
Briton had opted for a pair of Browning Hi-Power 9 mm handguns, and that he also planned to carry an M-4 assault rifle fixed
with a grenade launcher into battle.

Bolan slipped on his own gloves.

A voice buzzed in his earpiece.

"We'll be in position in thirty seconds," Grimaldi said. "I'm
going to drop you two off and hit the friendly skies, as per Sarge's
orders."

Though Grimaldi could carry more than his weight in a fight,
Bolan had ordered him to grab some distance from the drop site
as quickly as possible. Mauldin's intelligence had been good,
particularly when it came to building layouts and profiles of the
various players. But data on antiaircraft capabilities had been
scant. The Executioner was sure an arms dealer with Chernkova's reach had shoulder-fired rockets on the premises, if not in
an armory and immediately accessible. Bolan wasn't willing to
put a friend's life on the line just so he had an escape flight immediately handy. Besides, Grimaldi had another task to accomplish before he sought temporary cover, Bolan reminded himself.

The soldier moved the H&K submachine gun from where it
hung across his back so that it rested in front of his stomach, the
pistol grip within easy reach.

The helicopter cruised over the perimeter fence and hovered
in midair. Bolan and McCarter tossed the ropes from the cabin
door and watched them uncoil, stopping within feet of the hard-
packed earth below. The rope gripped in both hands, Bolan lowered himself onto the landing skids, while McCarter crouched
inside the cabin, the M-4 in his hand, barrel sweeping the ground
for threats. The soldier jumped from the landing skids, hands
gripping the rope, legs wrapped around it. The rotor wash pushed
down hard on him, caused the rope to swing and the fabric of
his clothes to ripple.

Before he'd covered half his descent, Bolan spotted a pair
of thugs emerging from the corner of a squat, one-story building—one of several dotting Chernkova's stronghold. One of the

men skidded to a halt, raised a gun-filled hand, drew a bead on the soldier.

Before the gunner could squeeze off a shot, McCarter's M-4 rattled. The compact assault rifle rained down death from above. A swarm of rounds stopped the guard in his tracks, stitching a diagonal line from groin to shoulder, the onslaught jerking the man's body in a final death dance.

Before the first gunman crashed to the ground in a dead heap, McCarter already had turned his weapon on the second shooter. McCarter aimed for center mass on the guy and a volley of bullets slammed into his torso. The slugs shredded the fabric of the man's coat and he let loose with a pained cry.

The guard backpedaled, tripping over a stone that jutted from the ground. But almost as soon as he'd hit the ground, Bolan caught sight of the first man trying to prop himself up on one elbow. A jagged muzzle flash flared from the man's assault weapon, but only managed to cut through empty air. Bolan guessed the guy wore body armor beneath the heavy jacket that covered his torso.

Bolan dropped into a crouch and squeezed off a punishing volley from the H&K submachine gun. The bullets tore into the downed shooter's legs, chewing up fabric, flesh and bone. The man cut loose with a scream that was audible even with a helicopter thrumming overhead. The guard, injured, mind and body seized by a primal urge to survive, answered Bolan's onslaught with another burst from his own weapon. The response was a muted one, the fast-aimed fire whizzing over Bolan's head. The soldier squeezed off a fast burst from the H&K, the slugs drilling into his opponent's head and shoulders.

Motion from the corner of his eye caught Bolan's attention. He wheeled left and spotted three more gunmen pouring through the door of another barracks. Bolan triggered the H&K. The weapon rattled out a murderous barrage. The man from blood swept the weapon in a figure-eight pattern. Slugs from the gun drilled into the soldiers, halted their advance, lanced through flesh and jerked them in a macabre death dance. The third man broke away from his dying comrades and sprinted for the cover of a black SUV

parked in front of the barracks. Bolan wheeled toward that man
and triggered the H&K again. The bullets pierced the shooter's
torso, the bullets tearing through his flesh. The gunman crashed
to the ground in front of the door to the barracks.

Glass burst out from one of the barrack's windows. The black
muzzle of an assault rifle poked through the window frame. The
weapon flared to life and bullets chewed into the ground, causing
geysers of dirt to erupt skyward. Bolan swung the H&K toward
this latest opponent, the SMG crackling through the rest of the
40-round magazine. The bullets punched through the window
glass and an instant later the gun fell silent. The soldier ejected
the 40-round magazine from the H&K weapon, practiced hands
searching out a fresh one from his web gear while icy eyes surveyed his surroundings.

Even as he fed another magazine into the weapon, Bolan saw
the barrel of another assault rifle jut through the window. He noticed that a grenade launcher was fixed underneath the barrel,
and the launcher's wide opening was swinging in his direction.

A SHOOTER SPRINTED OUT from behind a concrete-block building to McCarter's right. The stubby black submachine gun the
guy cradled spit a line of fire at the Briton, steel-jacketed slugs
pounding into concrete inches from his feet. McCarter squeezed
the M-4's trigger. A short burst caught the man in midstride and
spun him halfway around.

Before the dead man collapsed to the ground, McCarter was
already on the move, eyes sweeping his surroundings for more
threats. The roar of the helicopter's engines swelled from above.
Rotor wash stirred up small bits of dirt and gravel. McCarter
squinted to repel the pieces of debris pelting his face. He wished
for a moment that he'd worn goggles as Grimaldi had suggested,
realized he'd resisted as much to needle his old friend as for any
other reason.

Before he could regret the decision too much, the war bird had
slid forward without gaining additional altitude.

Another mechanical growl registered with the Briton. Wheel-
ing toward the sound, he spotted the chrome front grill of a

black sedan coming into view. The car surged out from behind a two-story building believed to house Chernkova's offices. Flames spat from the muzzle of a pistol that was pointing out from the passenger-side window. McCarter swept the assault rifle in a short horizontal arc. Bullets struck the vehicle's hood and sparked. Spiderwebs formed on the windshield, but didn't pierce it. Another burst emptied the M-4, but left the oncoming sedan unscratched.

An armored car, McCarter thought. And aren't I the lucky one?

The vehicle's power plant growling, it bore down on McCarter. Though his mind screamed for him to move from its path, he stood fast for as long as possible. Finally, when the vehicle's grill was a dozen or so feet from him, McCarter thrust himself to the side.

His performed a belly flop on the concrete. The impact stole his breath and might have broken a rib were it not for his ballistic vest. A curse exploded through clenched teeth. He maneuvered himself into a roll and grabbed some distance between himself and the vehicle, which roared past him.

The sedan's brake lights flared and the car slammed to a halt. McCarter maneuvered himself onto his belly. He brought around the assault rifle and triggered the grenade launcher. The HE round hissed from the launcher and struck the cracked concrete that lay beneath the vehicle's gas tank.

An explosion rent the air. Orange-yellow fire lashed out from beneath the vehicle. The force shoved the back end of the car several feet in the air before gravity yanked it crashing back to earth.

By that time, McCarter had reloaded the grenade launcher and was drawing a bead on the sedan.

Before he could trigger the weapon, though, an object hurtled down from the heavens and hammered into the vehicle's trunk. An ear-shattering explosion tore through the air. The force twisted the sedan's steel frame, and a fireball ripped through the car's interior. The force of the explosion yanked the vehicle several feet in the air before it turned on its side in midair and crashed back to the ground.

A voice sounded in McCarter's earpiece.

"Hellfire missile," Grimaldi said, satisfaction obvious in his voice.

"Nice work, lad," McCarter replied.

He grabbed a clip for the M-4 from his web gear and reloaded the weapon before hauling himself to his feet.

McCarter moved to the nearest building, one of those believed to be a barracks for Chernkova's security force. According to Mauldin's intelligence briefing, Chernkova kept all but a small cadre of security men at arm's length, making them eat and sleep in buildings away from him. Apparently the moron was worried he was worth actually becoming the target of a palace coup.

Well, he was half right. He was a target. Just because you're paranoid doesn't mean no one's out to get you, McCarter thought.

The Briton edged along the building's exterior, the M-4 raised to his shoulder.

His combat sense began ringing, prompting the soldier to shoot a glance skyward. Just as he did, he spotted a pair of hardmen creeping along the roof of another building to his right. The first man gripped a black handgun and he was pointing at something in the sky that was beyond McCarter's field of vision.

The other man balanced a rocket-propelled grenade on his shoulder. He appeared to be aiming it skyward, also. A cold sensation raced down McCarter's spine.

The bastard planned to shoot Grimaldi from the sky!

McCarter sighted down the M-4's barrel and squeezed off a quick burst from the assault rifle. The initial volley of bullets sailed past the face of the man with the grenade launcher. McCarter bit off a curse and readjusted his aim. In the meantime, the man with the handgun wheeled in McCarter's direction and punched off a couple of rounds from his handgun. The bullets whizzed pass McCarter's left ear and pounded into the concrete-block wall at his six.

McCarter punched out a burst from his assault rifle. The man with the pistol caught the swarm of 5.56 mm slugs in the head, the onslaught driving him from view. At the same time, the man with the RPG swung his weapon in McCarter's direction, the unfired projectile tracking in on the Phoenix Force commander.

Bloody hell, he thought.

15

Bolan saw the grenade launcher's muzzle locking in on him. Acting on instinct, the Executioner aimed the MP-7 at the window and triggered a sustained burst from the weapon. Rounds stabbed through the window and chewed into its frame. The launcher pitched through the glass, falling to the ground below.

Bolan ejected the empty magazine from the MP-7's grip, tossed it aside and grabbed another from his web gear. Before he could slide the new magazine into the submachine gun, he caught the sound of footfalls pounding against the earth. In the same fluid motion, he reloaded the H&K and whirled toward the sound. He caught the vague impression of a man dressed from head to toe in blue bearing down on him, arms outstretched, a knife gleaming in one hand.

Before the soldier could react, his opponent slammed into his stomach. Air exploded from Bolan's lungs and he staggered a couple of steps back. Before he could regain his footing, his assailant's weight pushed him too far back and caused him to plummet to the ground. The hardman landed on top of Bolan, pinning the soldier between himself and the concrete. The pressure on Bolan's chest and stomach forced him to belch out the contents of his lungs and restricted his ability to refill them.

The man drew back his fist and let it fly. Bolan whipped his head to the side to avoid the blow. The move saved him from the full impact of the punch, though the thug's knuckles managed to brush off the Executioner's cheek—painful but not the bone-crushing injury the man likely was capable of dealing out.

A wide grin spread over the other man's lips. He rained down two more fast jabs at the soldier's face. Bolan, able to again draw breath, batted aside an oncoming fist with a sweep of his arm. The impact of his forearm colliding with his assailant's wrist caused a flash of sharp pain before the lower part of his arm went numb. Throwing his other arm up, Bolan deflected the second punch, which only seemed to frustrate the man. His pale skin was sweat-streaked and mottled with patches of red.

The soldier drove an open hand into the man's solar plexus, driving the strike up at an angle. The stricken man gasped and threw another punch at the warrior. Bolan knocked aside the punch with his forearm. In the same motion, he drew up his right leg and his right hand stabbed down for the Beretta stowed in the thigh holster. Fingers wrapped around the pistol's grip, Bolan yanked the weapon free and shoved it into his opponent's mid-section and squeezed the trigger. A burst of 9 mm rounds drilled into the man's gut. Warm blood sprayed onto Bolan's hand. The man's body stiffened and his face went slack. He teetered for a heartbeat before Bolan shoved him aside and climbed to his feet.

In his other hand, Bolan grabbed the Desert Eagle that had been stowed away in the shoulder leather, thumbing back the hammer on the weapon.

Three more hardmen advanced on the soldier. Two of them brandished Kalashnikov rifles, while a third hung a few paces behind, clutching a pistol in one hand and a two-way radio in the other.

The Beretta and the Desert Eagle fired in unison, delivering a punishing hail of death. The triple-round bursts of 9 mm bullets lanced into the chest of the guard to Bolan's right. The rounds hit too high and to the left to strike the heart, but the sudden injury caused the man to drop his assault rifle and stumble forward. His now-empty hands flew to his chest and he covered the wound. A second burst from the Beretta drilled into the injured man's forehead. The force stopped his advance, twisting him forty-five degrees before his knees turned rubbery and he plummeted to the ground.

In the same instant, the Desert Eagle thundered twice, punch-

ing rounds into the wide forehead of the second shooter wielding
an AK-47, the slugs drilling into the bone just above the man's
thick eyebrow. The impact of the .44 rounds caused the top of
his head to disintegrate, leaving him with only enough brains to
realize he'd just lost a death match before his body went slack
and crumpled to the ground. The third man was already react-
ing, his pistol's muzzle tracking in on Bolan. The shooter's gun
barked out a couple of rounds that sizzled past Bolan's cheek.
The Desert Eagle responded with another peal of thunder, the
slug drilling through the man's sternum before ripping through
the other side of his torso in a spray of blood and gore.

Bolan holstered the Desert Eagle, just as bullets slammed into
the concrete several inches in front of his feet. The soldier darted
to his right and looked for the source of the shots. He spotted two
more hardmen crouched behind a midnight-blue pickup truck
parked twenty yards or so away. The two men had taken cover
behind the front end of the truck, apparently using the engine
block sealed inside as additional cover. Even as Bolan moved,
the Beretta was chugging through the rest of the clip, littering the
ground with shell casings. Slugs pierced the truck's steel hide,
stitching a ragged line of bullet holes in the vehicle's front fender.

The big American stowed the Beretta and scooped up one of
the discarded AK rifles that lay on the ground. Curling his finger around the AK's trigger, he started for the truck. One of the
shooters popped up from behind the hood. Triggering the Russian assault rifle, Bolan swept the AK-47 in a tight horizontal arc
as it spat a blistering barrage of bullets, littering the ground with
spent shell casings. The onslaught flayed the flesh of the guard's
face and arms, killing him. The second hardman snapped into
view, curling himself around the front end of the truck, his head
and part of his upper torso exposed as he tried to draw a bead on
Bolan with a Steyr AUG. The Stony Man warrior punched him
down with burst from the AK-47.

Bolan's assault rifle was nearly empty. His H&K was lost at
least a dozen yards back. He tossed aside the AK and grabbed
the fallen man's Steyr. A glance at the translucent magazine told
him the weapon was about half full. A pouch that hung from the

fallen hardman's shoulder held several more curled magazines for the weapon. Bolan freed the pouch's strap from the dead man's shoulder and slipped it on. The soldier didn't like using a weapon when he hadn't had a chance to at least field-strip and inspect it, but he had no time for that.

He needed to find Chernkova before the man tried to slip away. But first he needed to check in with McCarter.

I'LL NEVER MAKE IT! The thought careened through McCarter's head as he maneuvered the assault rifle to take out the man wielding the rocket-propelled grenade. An explosion—too loud for a grenade—tore through the air. Light flashed from behind the building in front of McCarter, dull enough to indicate it was a couple dozen yards away easily. Several smaller explosions followed quickly after that.

The sudden noise caused McCarter's opponent to hesitate in firing the RPG. McCarter used the time to his advantage. His M-4 churned through the contents of the clip. The 5.56 mm slugs drilled into the man wielding the rocket-propelled grenade, stitching a line from the man's hip to his shoulder. McCarter assumed the explosion meant Grimaldi had succeeded in his mission, firing a Hellfire missile into one of the armories where Chernkova stored his merchandise.

Dead fingers released the RPG. The weapon and its owner tumbled from the roof to the ground.

Another hard rain of gunfire erupted from McCarter's left. Bullets ripped into concrete several inches from his feet and spurred him into motion. He darted sideways to remove himself from the bull's-eye. Reloading on the run, he sized up his latest adversaries—a pair of shooters moving several feet apart from each other, unloading AK assault rifles on him. McCarter fired a frag grenade at the shooters. The round exploded and the swarm of razor wire from the grenade ripped through flesh and brought their advance to a sudden, bloody halt.

McCarter thumbed another round into the launcher. Several shooters, fewer than half a dozen, broke from cover. One of them turned toward the Briton. The guard's submachine gun was spitting flame and lead, but the fast burst flew harmlessly over Mc-Carter's head. He put the man down with a burst from his M-4. By then the others had disappeared from view, apparently headed toward the explosion site.

"McCarter?" Bolan's voice sounded in his earpiece.

"Go."

"Sitrep."

"Upright and kicking tail. Yourself?" McCarter asked.

"Same."

"Looks like Grimaldi came through for us."

Grimaldi chimed in to the radio traffic. "You sound surprised."

"Not surprised, lad. Just pleased. You saved my arse with that little stunt."

"Life's full of unintended consequences," Grimaldi replied.

"You're all heart."

CHERNKOVA HEARD THE unending carnage unfolding outside the steel door of his panic room—the explosions, the gunfire, the cacophony of fire and security alarms. And he felt terror squeeze his gut, his heart.

What should he do? Chernkova thought, with panic starting to seep in. He'd taken every security step imaginable, yet they weren't working. With each passing moment, his attackers moved closer. Heat radiated from his back, neck and chest like a bonfire and prompted him to remove his jacket and toss it aside. He moved to a pair of laptop computers that stood side by side on a folding table in the small sealed room. They'd been set up to provide footage from the various security cameras arrayed throughout the property. At least this way, he could see the bastards coming before they got here.

A glance at the screens caused his heart to skip a beat. The light blue background of his computer's desktop screen, the various folders and program windows were all gone. Instead the screens had turned into barren black fields broken only by a single word in white, block capital letters: DEAD.

The letters would disintegrate, one after the other, before re-forming again.

Chernkova swallowed hard and jumped up from his chair, knocking it over in the process. He wasn't scared, he told himself as he stumbled across the small room to where a steel gun locker stood, door ajar. He'd prepared for this. He'd prepared himself. He had.

Reaching into the locker, he drew out an Uzi. As he fed a 20-round magazine into the gun's pistol grip, more gunfire erupted right outside his door. His stomach plummeted and his hands moved jerkily while he worked the action on the submachine gun.

Screw this, he told himself. He wasn't sure what these bastards wanted or why they'd come for him. But he wasn't going down without a fight.

"Do you think the whole 'DEAD' thing was too much?" Kurtzman asked while staring into one of the computer monitors on his desk at Stony Man Farm.

Price, who was standing behind him, smirked. "That you only took it that far shows remarkable restraint," she said.

"A virus is no good if you can't add a personal touch," he said, shrugging. "Of course, if they ever track it, they're going to think it was sent by some little Jihad group in Indonesia, thanks to a little digital slight of hand."

Price patted her old friend on the shoulder. "You are a wizard," she said.

"If I was a wizard," Kurtzman said, "I'd conjure up a bonus."

"So you could afford a pointy hat? Get ready. I think Striker will need us again in a couple of minutes."

Bolan descended the stairs, the H&K held at the ready.

If Mauldin's information turned out to be good, and so far it had, Chernkova had a secure room in the basement of this building. Judging by the resistance he'd encountered as he'd entered the structure, Bolan had to believe that was the case.

The warrior set his left foot on the final step and hesitated. He was operating under the assumption that Chernkova would keep some people close by. The man was too big a coward to fight for himself or to walk five feet without a wall of gunners between him and the outside world. Bolan had skimmed the psychological profile provided by Mauldin, a ten-page document penned by some psychologist in Virginia.

It had identified Chernkova as a narcissist with paranoid tendencies. Bolan didn't need a doctor to tell him that. Most of the blood merchants he chased were narcissists, people willing to climb a hill of dead bodies to make a buck, but scared of their own shadows. That didn't make them easy to take down. An animal always fights at its fiercest when cornered, Bolan knew.

So, yes, he had Chernkova within his grasp, but he didn't have him.

Yet.

The soldier edged up to the corner and peered around it. A wide corridor stretched ahead of him. Steel mesh trays filled with thick bundles of cabling hung from the ceiling. Big round pipes hooked into the building's plumbing and climate-control systems ran the length of the ceilings. Occasionally, a small motor would kick on, drowning out any conversation with an irritating mechanical whine.

Bolan counted four guards standing at the ready. Two guarded a smooth steel door at the end of the corridor, one on each side. Two others had positioned themselves at other points along the corridor, assault rifles held at the ready.

Bolan drew back from view immediately. Holding the H&K by its pistol grip, he used his free hand to grab a flash-bang grenade from his web gear. Pulling the pin with his teeth, he tossed the device around the corner. A white flare illuminated the corridor, accompanied by a loud, disorienting crack.

A guard who'd been farthest from the small explosion spotted Bolan as he emerged from the stairwell. The guy swung up his assault rifle, but Bolan put him down with a fast burst from the H&K. He then took down the other three security men as they struggled to regain their senses after the blast from the stun grenade.

Sensing a presence at his six, the soldier whipped around. He saw McCarter stranding behind him. He greeted the Phoenix Force commander with a nod.

They moved for the door. Bolan studied it for a moment, saw it was sealed with a card-swiping system. He turned to McCarter, who was already moving to one of the fallen guards. He knelt next to the dead man, rolled the guy onto his back and searched through one, then the other breast pocket of the man's shirt. He stopped and held up a white card with a magnetic strip running down one side.

Hauling himself to his feet, McCarter handed the card to Bolan. The soldier took it and waited while McCarter slipped a pair of night-vision goggles over his eyes.

Bolan keyed the microphone. "Lights," he said.

Everything went black. Bolan slipped on his own NVGs, hoped the security system ran on a different circuit and dragged the card through the reader.

THE LIGHTS WENT OUT, replaced by an impenetrable blackness. Chernkova felt his stomach plummet. He held his breath and waited for the backup lights to switch on, counting to ten in his head. The lights never came on. The gunshots outside the door had faded away a minute or more before everything went dark.

A sick feeling seized his gut and blood thundered in his ears. If his people had ended up on the winning side of the skirmish outside his door, Chernkova knew they would have alerted him, told him he could relax. Their silence told him he stood alone.

He heard a mechanical hiss. The doors were opening.

BOLAN GRABBED ONE of Chernkova's forearms and spun the man around. He slammed an open palm into the space between the Russian's shoulder blades. The blow caused Chernkova to stumble forward without falling to the ground. He caught himself just as the lights came back on and wheeled around toward Bolan, right hand balled into a fist. He threw a punch at Bolan's gut. The Executioner leaned back slightly and let Chernkova's knuckles brush through empty air. A heartbeat later, the soldier's fist shot out and connected with Chernkova's rib cage. Bones snapped under the impact. The arms smuggler's eyes bulged. He belched out the contents of his lungs and stumbled back a couple of steps. He wrapped his arm protectively over his injured ribs. His face was flushed red and a sheen of perspiration filmed his forehead.

Bolan unsheathed the Beretta and leveled it at the bridge of the other man's nose.

"Hoped we could do this the easy way," Bolan said. "Apparently not."

"Easy, hell," Chernkova said. "You're going to kill me."

Bolan shrugged slightly. "Nothing hard about that. Ask your security team."

Chernkova tried to straighten up, but the movement sparked pain in his ribs and caused him to wince.

"You don't scare me," he said.

"Not even a little?" Bolan asked. "Then you're a fool."

"Who the hell are you? You come in here and destroy my life's work, everything I built with sweat and toil."

"And innocent blood," Bolan said. "Enough of that to fill a couple of oil tankers."

"That what this is about?" Chernkova asked. "You want a pound of flesh. I do something to you? Maybe something to your family?"

A smile ghosted Bolan's lips. "You overestimate yourself. Twenty-four hours ago, I'd never heard of you. Twenty-four hours from now, I won't remember you existed. Looking forward to that, frankly."

Chernkova licked his lips. He kept his arm folded protectively over his broken ribs. Bolan saw that he winced any time he took a deep breath. His eyes darted from Bolan to McCarter and back to the Executioner. He was sizing up the two men. The Russian finally locked his gaze on Bolan.

"You came here for a reason," Chernkova said. "You want something. I don't know what, but you came here for a reason. I have something you want. Am I right?"

"You're a genius."

"Tell me what it is. I'll get it for you. This doesn't have to go badly for any of us."

Bolan looked at McCarter. The latter met Bolan's gaze and shrugged.

The Executioner turned his face back toward Chernkova and pinned him with a stare. "There's no *us* in here," Bolan said. "Get that through your head. There's just you. You're all alone and you're screwed. Just how screwed depends on whether or not you give us what we want."

"Which is?"

"Information."

Chernkova smiled and nodded his head vigorously. "Information? If that's all you wanted—"

Bolan cut him off. "Not all," the soldier said. "Consider it a down payment."

"On?"

"Keeping your miserable existence."

"Of course. Anything you need."

"We'll get to that. For right now, though, just answer a question. You ran several shipments to a man, a Russian, in the last forty-eight hours. Where did you take them?"

Chernkova hesitated. Bolan guessed where the guy's mind was going and knew it was time to bring him back to reality.

"I know what you're thinking," Bolan said. "You're thinking, you don't want to give up Yezhov because he'll kill you. He'll hunt you down and murder you. Or, more likely, I'll have some other bloodthirsty bastard come for you."

Bolan paused a couple of seconds. Chernkova opened his mouth and Bolan silenced him with a gesture.

"Shut. Up. Anyway, I can't argue with that. If Yezhov was here right now, he'd kill you. No question. But here's the thing—he's not here. He's somewhere else. You need to worry about me and my friend here. Because, in case you haven't noticed, we also will kill you. Your security team would attest to that—if they could. Unfortunately, they've caught a severe case of dead and are a little short on insight."

Bolan brought his head down and leveled his gaze at Chernkova. "You understand me?"

Chernkova nodded, the movement small and resigned.

"Yezhov has a compound. It used to be a bear-hunting lodge, but it shut down many years ago."

"Where is it?" the soldier asked.

The Russian muttered the coordinates. The Executioner committed them to memory and he guessed McCarter did likewise.

McCarter broke his silence. "What did you take there?"

"Ammunition and weapons, but also food and other provisions. I think he's planning to be there for a little while. I wasn't sure why. He has several places around the world, each as nice as the last. The resort is a shit-hole. But it's well built and protected. He has three rings of walls around the main house. We had to land the planes outside those rings. He has light antiaircraft capabilities. MANPADS. And though his radar capabilities are rudimentary at best, mostly for supporting the airstrip operations, he does have them."

"Keep going," Bolan said.

"We still had one more shipment going to him. Mostly bullshit. He has three Italian sports cars, and some antique hunting rifles that have been in his family for decades."

"Where's the plane?"

"It's in our west hangar, already loaded," Chernkova said.

"Give me the tail number."

Chernkova reeled it off and Bolan made a mental note of it.

"You did good," the warrior said.

During the intervening silence, Chernkova fidgeted in his chair, before saying, "You didn't have to do all this."

"All what?" the Executioner asked.

Chernkova made a sweeping gesture at the room around them, but Bolan guessed it was meant to encompass much more.

"All this," he said, scarlet splotches reappearing on his neck. "Flying in here, killing my security team. Destroying one of my warehouses. I spent years building all this and you destroyed it in a matter of hours."

"Good work that," McCarter said.

"Fuck you. I'm trying to say it didn't have to go this way. I would have told you what you wanted without you doing all this."

"Somehow," Bolan said, "I doubt it. Call me a cynic, but I

think two hours ago you were feeling like the master of the universe. Two hours ago, you would have told us to go screw ourselves, and probably tried to kill us. But, now that your whole world's in flames and your back's against the wall, you're all about compromise."

Chernkova looked furious. "Just drop it," he said, forcing the words through clenched teeth.

"One more thing," Bolan said. "Maybe you're right. Maybe you would have spilled everything you knew without us dropping a hammer on you, I doubt it, but let's pretend that's true. Well, tough. I looked at your record. You have shipped weapons to backwater civil wars everywhere. Put guns in the hands of twelve-year-olds who were killing and raping villagers because the kids were jacked up on cocaine forced into their bodies by some psychopath warlord. And, given the chance, you'd be doing the same thing this afternoon."

Bolan paused for a couple seconds, considering his words.

"Here's the point," he said. "Maybe you and I could have struck a deal. Maybe I could have flown in here with suitcases filled with millions of dollars in cash. Maybe. But, frankly, I'd just as soon fly in here and burn your little operation to the ground, like we did. Oh, and you're penniless, too, by the way."

"What do you mean?"

"I mean your bank accounts," Bolan said. "They're frozen. Maybe you can get your buddies at the Kremlin to apply some diplomatic pressure, get them unfrozen. That shouldn't take more than a year or two."

"You bastard!" Chernkova shouted.

Bolan shaped his right hand like a gun, aimed the extended forefinger at the Russian and dropped the thumb. Deep furrows formed in Chernkova's forehead, telegraphing his confusion.

"Body's dead," Bolan said. "Head just doesn't know it yet."

The soldier turned on a heel and headed for the door. McCarter fell in behind him.

Enraged, Chernkova jumped up from his chair, knocked it to the floor. With a growl he lunged at the table, grabbed one of the Kimber handguns and swung up his shooting hand.

Bolan wheeled around, the Desert Eagle in his grip. A thunderclap filled the room and a large red hole opened in Chernkova's chest. The boat-tail slug shoved him back. As he tumbled backward, his forefinger tightened on the trigger and the gun cracked. A single round drilled into one of the computer monitors. The arms smuggler crashed to the floor in a heap.

16

The muffled beep of someone working the keypad outside her cell door registered with Davis. The locking bolt slid back. Her stomach plummeted with fear and her heart began to race. The door opened and revealed two guards. One of them, a tall, lanky man with straw-blond hair, marched through the door.

"Come," he said.

When she hesitated, his hand snaked out. Steely fingers wrapped around her biceps and he yanked her to her feet. The urge to knee him in the groin flared inside her. Before she could, though, he spun her around and shoved her against the wall. By then, the second guard, short and muscular, his head bald and lumpy, had stepped inside her cell. The two men wrestled her wrists together and handcuffed her, the cold steel rings biting into the skin of her wrists.

"You bastards!" she yelled. "Let me go!"

One of the men laughed. Thick, rough fingers grabbed the back of her neck and turned her toward the door, propelling her through it with a hard shove.

The guards led her through a series of corridors. With each step, the thundering of her heartbeat in her ears grew louder until she swore it drowned out all other sounds, save for the thudding of the guards' footsteps.

They reached a smooth steel door. She felt the grip on her neck loosen. When the hand drew away, the air cooled the sweat that had gathered under her captor's grip. The bald man came around from behind and jabbed a series of numbers into the keypad. When the lock gave way, he fanned open the door and stepped aside. A flat palm pounded her back, just between the shoulder blades, and she stumbled through the door. The guards followed her in.

A big man wearing a crisp white shirt, open at the collar, black slacks and black wingtip shoes stood inside. His thick arms were crossed over his massive chest. A thrill of fear raced through her as she realized the man was Yezhov. She recognized him from the pictures she'd found on the internet.

His small eyes followed her as she entered. The bald guard guided her to a folding chair and pushed her into it. She felt the cold steel seat and back pressing through her clothes, chilling her.

The well-dressed man unfolded his arms and closed the distance between them. He stopped a couple of feet from her, crossed his arms again and stared down at her. The starched fabric of his shirt made a scratching noise as his arms moved. His eyes didn't seem to blink. She detected traces of his cologne in the air.

"It's been a long chase," he said. "A long and tiring one. And expensive, too. Let's not forget that. You've cost me a small fortune."

Davis silently stared down at her lap. He reached his right hand out and grabbed her chin. Making a pincer of his forefinger and thumb, he squeezed her chin hard and tilted her face up. His dead eyes studied her for several seconds.

"You're smaller than I expected," he said, finally. "Pretty, probably beautiful if you did something with yourself."

His grip eased and she jerked her head away. His lips twisted into an ugly smile as he stepped back from her.

"Now, your sister, she was—" he stared up at the ceiling and rubbed his chin, as though searching for the right word "—beautiful, glowingly so. Of course, that happens when you have something growing inside you. She had something growing inside her, correct?"

She heard one of the guards guffaw from behind.

The fear evaporated and her muscles tensed with anger.

"You son of a bitch," she growled through clenched teeth. Before she could think better of it, she shot up from the chair. A pair of open hands descended on her shoulders and shoved her back into the seat. The guard kept his hold on her shoulders and kept her pinned in the chair.

Yezhov stepped forward again. This time his face hovered six inches or so from hers. His breath felt hot against her cheek. The expensive cologne did nothing to cover the rotting-meat quality of his breath, as though death were bundled inside him, making up his core. She returned his unyielding stare. It was obvious to her that he saw her only as an obstacle, a thing that stood between him and the latest shiny object he coveted.

The eyes alternately chilled and angered her. He hadn't killed her sister, but someone like him had. A man out for a payday, one glad to wipe out whole families for a few dollars in his bank account or some extra points in an ideological battle. She'd been fighting bastards like Yezhov for years, hitting them where she believed it hurt most, in the wallet, always striking quickly and surreptitiously. They never saw her coming, which was how she liked it. But this time, faced with evil, when she should have been scared, she was just pissed.

"My dear," he was saying, "you have an anger problem. It needs to be fixed."

"Fix this," she said.

Gathering saliva in her mouth, she spit it at him. The glob of liquid splattered against his cheek. He screwed his eyes shut and reflexively drew his head back a few inches.

His face darkened and his open hand lashed out and struck her cheek. The force whipped her head hard to the right. She turned her gaze back on the Russian. He loomed over her, hand drawn back and ready to strike again. When his hand struck her face again, she ground her teeth together, unwilling to yelp with pain, to give the bastard the satisfaction. After another hit, he stepped back and studied her. The skin of his neck and cheeks, a deep scarlet, telegraphed his anger. Otherwise, his expression remained flat.

He turned and walked to a nearby table and picked up a white towel, which he used to mop the sweat from his forehead and neck. He tossed the towel back onto the table, turned halfway and looked at Davis.

"You are tough," he said. "I have a feeling you could take several more hits before you give in, tell me what I want to know."

"You haven't asked any questions."

"No, I suppose you're right. Consider this first part payback, a preview of what you can expect if you decide to tough it out."

He pointed a finger at her. "But I have something that I think will change your attitude."

He picked up a black rectangular device that she recognized as a tablet computer. Without looking at her, he crossed the room, moving in her direction while running his index finger over the computer's screen. He stopped a couple of feet from her, looked at the screen, smiled and turned it in her direction.

She gasped. On the screen was a short video of Maxine Young, shot from the waist up. She lay on her back on a bed. Her eyes were closed and her hair mussed. Davis could tell from watching her chest rise and fall that Young was breathing—at least for the time being.

Yezhov let her watch it for several seconds before he turned on a heel and carried the tablet back to the table.

Turning back around, he pinned her with his gaze.

"So I can continue to beat the hell out of you. Fine with me. And I'll kill your friend. Or you can answer my questions and save her life."

Davis squeezed her eyes shut and considered his words. It took only seconds to make a choice.

GRIMALDI'S VOICE BURST from speakers in the War Room at Stony Man Farm. Kurtzman was in his wheelchair at a bank of computers.

"We're almost in position," the pilot said. "Ready to do your thing?"

"You know I am," Kurtzman replied.

His fingers glided over the keyboard. He had broken through the firewalls of Yezhov's IT system. Windows continued to pop up and disappear on his screen as he burrowed deeper. When he found what he was looking for, he grinned. With a couple of keystrokes, he could shut down the main generators of Yezhov's stronghold, override the door locks and force them on to the weaker backup generators.

"Now?" he asked.

"Now," Grimaldi replied.

Kurtzman began punching buttons.

"YOU REALIZE THIS IS AN affront to decent men everywhere, don't you?" McCarter said.

"Just do it," Bolan replied.

"Bloody Americans," the Briton said. "You have no appreciation for beauty."

"Do it."

The two men stood in the cargo area of the plane, next to three Huayra sports cars parked in a pyramid formation. Two were silver, a third was red. While McCarter had slept, Bolan had wedged C-4 explosives around the fuel tanks of the cars. He carried the detonator in his left hand.

"They have gull-wing doors," McCarter said.

"Do it."

"Seven hundred horsepower. Put them together, it equals twenty-one hundred horsepower."

"Do it or I will."

McCarter lovingly grazed his fingertips along the surface of the red car's roof.

"We could keep one. Spoils of war and all that."

"You could ride one down, if you'd like," Bolan suggested.

"Fine, we dump them."

THE SENTRY STATIONED outside Yezhov's compound stared at the big cargo plane winging its way toward him. He keyed his throat microphone and told the operations center about the airplane.

"We know about it," the security coordinator said. "It's one of Chernkova's planes. They're bringing supplies. And the boss's cars."

"The Huayras?"

"Right."

"Okay."

The sentry shook his head in disbelief. Who the hell needed a million-dollar sports car—let alone three—in the middle of the damn wilderness? The desire for a cigarette began to gnaw at him and he forgot about the airplane.

The guard patted his pockets until he remembered he'd left his cigarettes in his room. He made an irritated noise and with the fingers of his right hand peeled back the cuff of his left sleeve exposing his watch. Another twenty-five minutes and he'd be off duty. He'd smoke his damn brains out then.

In the meantime, he shifted his gaze back to the plane, which had started to carve out a tight circle in the sky. This is what it all had come down to, watching a damn plane to pass the time. It was the closest thing to television they had. Any signals into and out of the facility were tightly controlled. Up here, his mobile phone was just a chunk of metal, glass, plastic and dead circuitry. It was either watch the bears or watch yet another supply plane land. If he was lucky, he might get a glimpse of one of the sports cars as they were unloaded. It was the closest he'd get to such a luxury, he thought.

A mechanical whirring caught his attention. He looked harder at the plane and noticed that the rear cargo ramp was cracking open as the plane nosed its way over the compound walls. He turned to watch it.

What the hell? None of the previous planes had used air drops for the supplies, that he could recall. And, knowing Yezhov's affinity for his cars, the sentry couldn't imagine someone convincing the Russian that parachutes and harnesses would be enough to deliver his precious toys to the ground.

The ramp was yawning open wider. The guard's fingers drifted toward the controls for his throat microphone. Before he could press a button, he saw a flash of motion on the ramp and a sleek shape suddenly appeared in the sky. One of the cars! The man could only stare in disbelief as the other two cars rolled from inside the plane in fast succession.

BOLAN STOOD AT the edge of the ramp and watched through his goggles as the cars plunged toward the ground. Both he and Mc-Carter had strapped on parachutes. For the infiltration, the Executioner had selected an M-4 assault rifle with an M-203 grenade launcher, along with his usual handguns and other equipment.

The wind roared past his ears, making it impossible to hear anything other than wind, plane engines and the doomsday numbers counting down in his head.

Three, two, one.

With his thumb, he flicked the switch on the detonator. A trio of orange fireballs blossomed below, a small, sudden serving of hell for Yezhov and his people. He advanced down the cargo ramp, the wind fiercely pushing back against his every step. When he ran out of ramp, he plunged into the nothingness, McCarter a couple of steps behind.

YEZHOV HEARD THE MUFFLED thumps through the fortified walls. Cursing, he pulled back the tip of the knife blade, which had hovered an inch or so from Davis's eye. He slipped the knife back into the spring-loaded holster strapped around his left forearm. When it clicked into place, he pulled his sleeve down over the weapon.

He gave her one last look. He drank in the swollen eye, the blood trickling from her bottom lip, the one he'd split open with his knuckles. The same blow had broken a tooth.

"I wish I could stay," he said. "Regretfully, I can't."

"Bite me," she said.

"Later, perhaps," he replied. By then, pandemonium had broken loose outside the room. Through the door, Davis could hear footsteps pounding and people shouting.

Yezhov followed his captive's gaze for a second, quickly whipped his face back toward her and pinned her with narrow eyes.

"If you brought all this on me," he said, "I'll do much worse."

He turned to the other Russian, the one who she was told had killed Young. Apparently the information Davis was feeding them wasn't enough for them to keep their word. They killed her friend anyway. Then they had showed her a picture of Young shot in the head—for their own amusement, she supposed.

The man's pale green eyes had monitored Davis's interrogation with freakish intensity, as though the process interested him a great deal more than her actual answers. He likely had been the one to question Young, too. His had been the last face the poor woman saw before she'd died. Just the thought caused a sick feeling to wash over Davis.

"Take our guest back to her room," Yezhov said.

Mikoyan nodded and turned his gaze toward her. Something flickered in the man's eyes and a chill raced through Davis. Apparently, Yezhov sensed something, too.

"I said, put her in her room," he said. "Grab a gun and fight."

Mikoyan nodded sullenly. His boss wheeled around and marched out the door.

The pasty-faced Russian moved up on Davis. His hand reached out. Her breath caught in her throat and she felt her body tense. Plunging his fingers into her hair, he grabbed a handful of it twisted violently and pulled up. A yelp of pain and surprise escaped her lips before she could stop it.

She had no choice but to come to her feet. The movement ignited a searing pain in her right rib cage that stole her breath. It emanated from a spot where Yezhov had driven a fist into her ribs during the interrogation. She ground her teeth together to keep from crying out in pain a second time. She wouldn't give Mikoyan the satisfaction of seeing her suffer.

Mikoyan didn't release her hair, but instead used it to guide Davis to the door, like a dog on a leash. His grip was so tight she couldn't move her head even slightly without igniting the sensation of dozens of needles jabbing into her skull simultaneously.

They moved into the hallway and he guided her back to her room, walking her at an excruciatingly slow pace. Armed men rushed past them in the halls.

When he reached the door, he punched a numeric code into a keypad fixed to the wall. The bolt slid aside and the door swung open. He shoved her inside. By the time she caught her footing and spun toward the door, it was closing.

"I'll be back for you," he said before he slammed the door shut.

17

Bolan, the M-4/M-203 grenade launcher held at the ready, advanced over the cracked pavement of the long-neglected parking lot, and made his way toward Yezhov's stronghold.

Minutes earlier, he and McCarter had landed inside the compound's multiple security walls, where they'd shed their parachutes and began their attack.

As Bolan had planned, mayhem heralded their arrival. The burning, twisted wreckages of expensive Italian sports cars had speared through the roofs of buildings. The explosions from the C-4 had unleashed a storm of burning tires, jagged glass and razor-sharp metal fragments. At least a dozen hardmen, either injured or dead, were strewn about the grounds before he or McCarter ever squeezed off a shot. Yezhov's soldiers poured from the main building, the former resort. A handful carried fire extinguishers while most were loaded down with Steyr AUG and old Soviet Union AKR submachine guns.

The soldier's plan was simple—break into the main building, burn down as many of Yezhov's people as possible and take out the big Russian himself. But Bolan's primary goal was to extricate Davis, even if he didn't make it out himself. He owed the woman that much.

Gunfire rattle emanated from Bolan's right. He turned his head toward the sound and glimpsed McCarter burning down a pair of Yezhov's shooters in a hail of gunfire.

A trio of gunmen advanced from Bolan's right. The soldier spun, fired a round from the launcher. The round struck the ground behind them and exploded. A maelstrom of metal fragments chewed into the men. The onslaught elicited a series of agonized screams as their mangled forms folded to the ground. Before the soldier could reload, the whine of an engine from his right caught his attention. He wheeled toward the sound. A handful of guards parted and a motorcycle burst through the space between them. A helmeted figure drove it, while a second rode on the back, the flames and smoke spitting from the muzzle of the pistol clutched in his hand.

Bolan held his ground and maneuvered the rattling M-4 in a figure eight. A ragged line of bullet wounds sprang open across the chest of the oncoming motorcyclist. Dead fingers released the grips of the handlebars. The front wheel cranked into a hard left angle, and the rear wheel fishtailed. Pulled down by the weight of two bodies, the bike tipped and fell into a sideways slide and skidded along the ground toward Bolan. The corpse of the gun-wielding rider was flung from the bike along the way.

The soldier thrust himself to the side, rolled when he hit the ground and came up on one knee, ice-blue eyes sweeping the terrain for more threats. A short volley from the M-4 took down two more of the hardmen.

As he rose to standing, Bolan loaded an HE round into the grenade launcher. He set his sights on a single-story building that stood a distance from him. The structure was made of concrete blocks, painted white. One of the cars had crashed through the top of the building, taking half the roof with it. The undulating glow of flames was visible inside the structure through the single-pane windows. A pair of bay doors that made up half of the building's front exterior were buckling from the onslaught of the flames. A circular drive populated by a pair of white Humvees lay in front of the garage.

A handful of Yezhov's soldiers who had been trying to hose down the structure abandoned the work when they saw Bolan, and began grabbing for pistols, assault rifles and submachine guns.

Another man was climbing frantically into the cab of a tanker truck with a mirrorlike finish. Judging by the man's urgency, Bolan guessed the truck wasn't filled with corn syrup.

He leveled the launcher and fired.

The HE round hissed forth from the launcher and drilled into the tanker. Thunder pealed. The tanker's skin swelled, then buckled before it burst outward. The explosion's force shoved the ass end of the tanker skyward and doused those closest to it with flaming liquid. One person, body engulfed in flames, burst into a run. Bolan brought the M-4 to his shoulder and punched a mercy round into the flaming figure's skull, ending his suffering.

Bolan turned on his heel and headed for the main building.

"Bloody hell," McCarter said. "Before you crack open hell's gate, a warning might be nice."

"My bad," Bolan said. "Give me a sitrep."

"I've taken down at least a dozen of these bastards," McCarter said. "I'd say we have a clear path to our Russian friend." He paused. "At least until we get inside the building. Then we can start this whole bloody dance over again."

"Whatever it takes," Bolan replied.

"WHAT DO WE DO?" Tatania Sizova asked.

"We fight," Yezhov said. He forced the words through clenched teeth. "Damn it, we fight."

Yezhov didn't look at his lover when he spoke. Peering through the window of their second-floor suite, his gaze was fixed on the carnage below. He saw two men—only two men—shooting their way across the landscape. He assumed one was this man Cooper. Both were slicing through his people with deadly efficiency.

He turned to Tatania. Her face was taut, pale, but he saw determination in her eyes. He knew she wouldn't fold; she'd go down fighting. She already had donned a loose-fitting black jumpsuit with black leather boots that reached halfway up her calf. A pistol belt was wrapped around her slim waist. Yezhov had donned similar garb. A pair of Steyr AUG subguns were laid out on the bed.

She closed the distance between them. Wrapping her arms around him, she pressed her body against his, leaned her head against his chest and sighed. Knowing they might find themselves in a fight, she'd ceased wearing makeup or perfume. But he still caught a faint whiff of her floral-scented soap.

She said, "And once we win, we'll have to run again."

"Yes, but not far," he replied. "The Russian government will protect us. We did this for them. They have no choice but to protect us."

"You believe this?"

"I know it."

"How can you be so sure?" Tatania asked.

"I kept excellent notes," he said, a faint smile on his lips. "I have videos, telephone transcripts, duplicate files. I spied on the spies. If the Russian government doesn't cooperate, their secrets will be mailed to the White House and other world capitals."

"And the satellite codes?"

"I have them on a flash drive. If extortion doesn't buy the Russians' help, surely the codes will."

She looked up at him and gave a tight smile. "I never should have doubted you."

"No, you shouldn't have," he said.

"You believe we can do this?"

"There are only two of them."

"They've gotten far," she said, "for just two."

"That means they're only that much closer to their luck running out," Yezhov replied.

CLOSING IN ON THE MAIN entrance, Bolan studied it. Though weathered, the pair of wooden doors that sealed the building from the outside looked formidable. If bolted from the inside, he guessed they wouldn't open without the help of explosives.

That there were no guards stationed outside them also bothered the warrior. He couldn't imagine Yezhov leaving the front unguarded. If Bolan and McCarter had eliminated Yezhov's security team, leaving no one else to guard the place, fine. But Bolan wasn't ready to jump to that conclusion, yet.

McCarter rejoined him and they walked about ten yards apart from one another as they closed in on the building.

McCarter's voice buzzed in Bolan's earpiece again. "Apparently, we've won."

"Apparently," Bolan replied.

"But without the parade."

"Right."

A driveway stretched in front of the building. A brick porch rose up about a foot from the ground and stood in front of the door. Bolan reached the edge of the porch, started to raise his foot, but checked himself.

"What's the matter?" McCarter asked.

"Just playing a hunch," Bolan said. "Stay away from the door and use a window."

"Roger that."

Bolan backtracked a dozen steps to a row of tall, single-pane windows that looked into a massive open room. The Executioner advanced on the window, the M-4 chattering in his hands. The 5.56 mm slugs punched through the glass and showered the ground with shards. Passing through the now-empty window frame, Bolan moved into what he assumed once had been a lounge area. The carpet closest to the windows was faded from sunlight and occasionally spotted by water leaks. A massive fireplace made up of gray stones rose up in the middle of the room. Graffiti—most of it in Russian, though he spotted occasional flourishes of English profanity—marred the walls and ceilings. It looked faded and Bolan assumed it predated Yezhov's decision to fortify the place.

Suddenly gunfire erupted elsewhere in the building. Bolan surged toward the sound of the shooting.

Exiting the lounge area, he followed a short corridor that led into a smaller room that Bolan assumed had served as a receiving area for guests. A glance at the front door confirmed his earlier suspicion that it had been wired to explode once it was opened. A check-in counter ran parallel to the rear wall of the room.

When he reached the exit door, he paused and peered through the door. A pair of Yezhov's thugs were firing at a target Bolan couldn't see. Judging by the bullet holes suddenly opening in the wall, someone was returning fire. Gun smoke clouded the air as the spent brass fell to the ground. The Executioner fired the M-4 and took down the man closest to him with a hail of bullets. The second shooter, now suddenly under attack from another direction, started to swivel in Bolan's direction. Before he could finish the move, the soldier's M-4 chewed open the man's chest.

Ejecting the spent magazine, Bolan slipped another into the assault rifle while moving through the door, while McCarter stepped through the window frame, its edges torn ragged from the gunfire. The two men slipped into the nearest corridor, with Bolan in the lead. Searching each of the rooms, they found and took down three more of Yezhov's guards before moving to the second floor. Bolan emerged from the stairwell. With the M-4 pressed snug against his shoulder, he crept along the wall. One of the Russian's gunmen stepped into view, his Steyr held at waist level. The submachine gun ground out a volley of bullets. The initial burst lanced past Bolan and McCarter. The man from blood's M-4 churned out a burst that shredded the man.

Two more guards emerged from other rooms lining the corridor. One was armed with a Steyr, the second with a SPAS shotgun. McCarter launched into action first, letting loose a hellstorm of gunfire that stitched the man from right groin to left shoulder.

Thunder pealed from the shotgun. The blast ripped into the floor several yards ahead of Bolan and McCarter. Bolan replied with a volley from the M-4 that punched through the man's thighs. The thug screamed and fell to the floor. The shotgun slipped from his grasp and clattered across the floor.

Bolan started toward the shooter, his assault rifle's muzzle centered on the man's back. The big American planned to shake the guy down for some intel about Davis's location. Kneeling next to the man, Bolan rolled the thug onto his back. Jaws clenched, face soaked with sweat, the man glared at Bolan and grabbed for a pistol strapped to his waist. Bolan poked the M-4's barrel into the guy's stomach and he froze. The soldier snatched the pistol from the man's hip holster and tossed it aside.

"The woman," Bolan said, "where is she?"

The thug hesitated. His defiant glare faded and his eyes

seemed to lose focus. Bolan noticed the man's skin growing pale quickly.

The pool of blood around them widened on the floor. The Executioner guessed one of his bullets had severed an artery and the man would bleed out quickly.

"Where is she?"

The man's mouth opened. In the same instant, Bolan heard the click of a door latch behind him.

"Look out!" McCarter shouted.

Bolan turned at the waist in time to see a man he recognized as Yezhov step into view. The Russian was drawing a bead on Bolan. McCarter ripped off a fast burst from his own submachine gun, but Yezhov surged into the hallway, the rounds just missing him, pounding into a wall instead.

A second black-clad figure stepped into the corridor. Bolan recognized her as Yezhov's lover. Her face a mask of determination, she was swinging the muzzle of her Uzi toward Bolan. He responded first, unloading a burst into her center mass. The look of determination drained away, replaced with wide-eyed shock. She stumbled back a couple of steps before colliding with a wall. Her knees buckled and she sank to the ground, leaving a wide, ragged crimson smear on the wall.

"No!" Yezhov shouted.

Instinctively, he took a step toward his fallen lover, halted. When he whipped his head toward Bolan and McCarter, his face was flushed with rage, eyes narrowed into slits. A primal howl burst from his lips. Vengeance blazed forth from the submachine gun he gripped.

The slugs just narrowly missed Bolan, but carved a jagged line in the wall just above his head.

Then the Russian darted through a pair of double doors. Bolan climbed to his feet. Reloading the M-4, he moved for the doorway. McCarter fell in behind him. From inside the stairwell, he could hear the thud of Yezhov's footsteps as he descended the stairs.

"I'll get him," Bolan said. "You find Davis."

McCarter nodded and Bolan headed through the doorway.

18

The electric lights winked out in Davis's room, plunging it into blackness. The locking bolt on her door snapped back with a thud and the door swung inward, the bolt being the only thing that had held it in place. After a couple of seconds of darkness passed, more subdued lighting blinked on. Though she couldn't hear one, Davis assumed a backup generator had fired up somewhere in the building.

When the door cracked open Davis had been sitting on her cot, gingerly touching her ribs to determine the extent of her injuries. Even the slightest pressure ignited white-hot needles of pain that caused her to draw in air sharply and grind her teeth—no doubt at least one of her ribs was broken, if not more. While her head throbbed from a punch to the side of the head from Yezhov that had opened a gash that was still trickling blood. And even though she'd spit blood onto the floor twice, its coppery taste still filmed her tongue.

When the door first parted from the frame, she tensed, expecting Mikoyan to enter. The man had promised to come back and God only knew what he had planned. She raised herself from the bed, hands curled into fists. The room had been stripped of any blunt objects she could use as weapons, but she still planned to fight, broken ribs, bloody head and all.

Seconds passed and no one entered the room.

With tentative steps, she moved toward the door. Grabbing the edge of it, she swung the door aside. The muffled rattle of gunfire was audible from the upper levels of the building. A smile twitched at her lips. Cooper's here, she thought. It had to be him. She had no idea how he'd found her, but she was grateful he was here.

If she had any sense, she told herself, she'd stay put and wait until he found her. But what if he didn't make it? It only took one well-placed bullet to put a man down. She could find herself facing Yezhov and Mikoyan again if she didn't take action.

Screw it, she told herself, it's time to move.

She peered around the door frame, but saw the corridor outside was empty. She stepped through the door. The movement caused bolts of pain to emanate from her ribs, but she ignored it as best she could. She edged along the wall and headed for the nearest stairwell.

Out in the hallway, unarmed, she felt exposed. The small hairs on the back of her neck prickled and her mouth felt hot and dry. An urge to go hide overtook her. This is crazy, a voice chided her. She thought of Maxine Young, thought of her hopping on a plane and crossing the Atlantic to lend a hand. She thought of Cooper coming to her aid, and the dozens of others who'd had her back over the past several years, and kept moving ahead, unwilling to fold.

She climbed the stairs slowly. When she reached the first-floor landing, the gunfire was louder, but still sounded like it was deeper in the building. Slowly, she pushed down on the door's release bar until it gave no more. She pushed the door open, peered through the crack. She saw several bodies littering the floor. She went through the door and closed it slowly behind her.

A man dressed in jeans and a black turtleneck lay on his back several yards from her. Groaning, he held both hands over his midsection, apparently trying to keep pressure on his wound. Blood seeped through the spaces between his fingers.

Closer to her, a pump shotgun outfitted with a pistol grip lay on the floor. Its former owner, his midsection ripped apart by bullets, lay on his side, completely still.

She crept toward the weapon. When it lay just a few feet out of her reach, motion ahead of her caught her attention. A burly man dressed in olive-green coveralls, body wrapped in military web gear, stepped from one of the rooms. He held a black pistol in one hand. Her stomach plummeted and she froze in midstride.

He appeared not to notice her. Perhaps he was more worried about helping his injured friend? With his back turned toward her, she started moving again, but kept an eye on the hardman.

As she closed the distance between her and the shotgun, she saw the man in green raise the pistol and point the muzzle at the fallen guard.

He muttered something sharp in Russian and the gun cracked once. The injured man's body jerked once as the bullet tunneled into his torso. The sudden and unexpected savagery of killing one of his own shocked Davis, who long ago assumed she'd lost the capacity for such a naive emotion. She gasped and the gunner who stood before her heard the noise. He whirled in her direction and snapped off a quick shot from his pistol.

Davis thrust herself forward. Her hands stabbed out and she grabbed hold of the shotgun, its grip sticky with blood. She swung the shotgun's barrel at her opponent. By this time, the man was tracking her with his pistol. As his finger tightened on the trigger, Davis unleashed a blast from her weapon that ripped into the man's chest. The onslaught from the shotgun shoved him off his feet and he smacked to the ground, dead.

Working the shotgun's slide, she chambered another round and rose up in a crouch. She didn't bother to wipe away the blood that smeared the shotgun's grip or her right palm. Her right hand gripping the weapon, she rested the slide on her knee, and with her free hand she patted down the corpse that lay next to her. She found a handful of shotgun shells in one of his pockets, and she slipped them into one of the side pockets on her jeans. Unclipping a holstered Browning Hi-Power from his hip, she attached it to the waistband of her jeans, and pocketed two magazines. Once she came to her feet, she fed a couple of fresh shells into the shotgun. A radio attached to his belt squawked. She considered taking that, too, but decided against. The voices emanating from it spoke Russian, a language she didn't understand. The noise likely would be more of a distraction than anything else, she decided.

The blood-splattered walls and rent flesh surrounding her began to seep into her consciousness. At the same time, her ribs continued to ache. She shoved all that aside and thought fleetingly of Young, her face marred by a bullet. Then Davis thought of her twin sister and her husband, their bodies charred and mangled in the train explosion. A niece she'd never hold.

Rage welled up inside her, sparking a surge of adrenaline that anesthetized the ache in her ribs, the throbbing in her skull. She still felt it on some level, the pain, the disgust, but she also felt separated from it, as though it were happening to someone else.

Giving the rooms a cursory look, she found them all empty. She quit the first floor and took the stairs to the second level, the shotgun angled upward. She found the door that led into the second floor held open by another corpse. The dead man lay in a pool of blood on his back, legs spread into a narrow V, the door pushing against one hip.

Elbowing the door open, she pushed it aside and moved through the door. The hinges groaned, setting her teeth on edge. A man was standing several yards away, speaking into a hand-held radio. The sound of the door caught his attention. He spun toward Davis and made a play for a pistol fixed to his right hip.

Before he could clear leather, Davis's shotgun roared once. The maelstrom unleashed from the weapon shredded the man's torso and thrust him off his feet. Even as the echoes of the blast died away, a second shooter appeared around a doorjamb a few yards away. He squeezed off a quick shot with his pistol. The bullet sizzled past Davis's ear. The shotgun she cradled thundered again.

The gun's fire shredded the man's face and his exposed arm. Mangled fingers let go of the gun and the hardman collapsed to the ground.

She worked the shotgun's slide again as she continued down the corridor.

The adrenaline coursed through her, dulling any pain or stiffness in her body. However, the roar from the shotgun had left an incessant ringing in her ears. She tried as best as possible to ignore it and keep going. She wanted to find Mikoyan.

She had taken maybe a half-dozen steps when the small hairs on the back of her neck prickled. The shotgun leading the way, she wheeled around. Before she'd turned even a quarter of the way, though, someone grabbed the gun's barrel and shoved it aside. The unexpected thrust knocked Davis off balance slightly.

She became aware of Mikoyan standing there, his hand gripping the pump-action shotgun's barrel with one hand to keep control of it. Before Davis could react, his other hand, fingers extended, lashed out. The back of his hand connected with her cheek. This time she rolled with it, like she had been taught to do. His knuckles brushed against her cheek. The blow stung. Then he miscalculated. Using just one hand, he tried to yank the shotgun from her grip, underestimating her strength. When the gun didn't give, he paused, only for less than a heartbeat. Long enough for Davis to reverse the barrel a few inches, directing the shotgun's snout toward his torso.

She squeezed the weapon's trigger. Jagged flames and buckshot exploded from the barrel. The blast ripped into his torso and he screamed, surrendered his grip on the shotgun and spun away.

Davis chambered another round and maneuvered the barrel toward Mikoyan again. The weapon roared, and with less than two feet between them, the rounds ripped open Mikoyan's midsection, and thrust him back a couple of feet before his body, the upper and lower halves nearly separated by the punishing blast, slammed to the floor. Mikoyan's blood had splattered onto Davis, staining her hands, her face and her clothes.

Seeing his corpse on the floor, she felt the steel in her own body drain away, replaced by light-headedness and rubbery knees. She stepped away from him until her back collided with a wall. She slid down the surface, bending at the knees, until her butt touched the floor. Whereas the first time she'd killed, she'd cried and felt as though she'd lost something precious, something she'd never regain, this time she only felt hollow and distant. It was as though she had watched the whole thing happen without participating in it herself.

Sure, she'd secured some measure of justice for Young. But the killing left her with no joy, no guilt, no anguish.

She felt nothing, as though her actions had no more significance than washing her hands.

Davis realized then that much of the shooting had subsided. She continued sitting on the floor, but began feeding more shells into the shotgun. When she finished, she set the shotgun on the floor next to her. She reached into her pants pocket with her thumb and index finger, felt around until she found the cell phone the Russians had given her, and drew it from her pocket. Using her thumb, she pressed a couple of buttons until she found the picture Mikoyan had taken of Young, stared at it for several agonizing seconds. Tears stung the corners of her eyes. Grief and anger constricted her throat. She swallowed hard and tossed the phone at the Russian's corpse. It landed in the space where his stomach once had been.

She then rose to her feet and started to walk away from Mikoyan's remains, without giving him a second glance.

"Burn, fucker," she muttered.

19

Yezhov surged into the pool room.

He looked the place over, hunting for somewhere to hide. The walls were smeared with graffiti. Overturned tables and chairs were arrayed around the room, having remained undisturbed since vandals had knocked them over. Water had seeped through the skylights and several inches of it had collected in a dark brown mixture at the pool's deep end. The air reeked of mildew.

A small tool shed stood in one corner of the room. Yezhov jogged to it and hid behind it. Reaching into the hip pocket of his pants, he withdrew two more shells and loaded them into the shotgun. He came around from behind the shed, the weapon held at the ready at hip level.

Two shadows moved through the door. He tensed until he recognized both as members of his private army. Walking along the edge of the pool, the three men met at its midpoint.

"Where are they?" Yezhov asked.

"Two are still pinned down on the second level," one of the men said.

"The American?"

"You mean the big guy with the black hair? Don't know." The guard shook his head to emphasize the point. "Maybe someone took him down."

Yezhov shook his head. "He's coming."

He scanned the room again. When his eyes lighted on the balcony, he paused and an idea formed in his mind. Yezhov turned back to the other two hardmen and held out his shotgun. "Trade me," he said.

The senior guard handed over his Kalashnikov and took away the shotgun. He then handed over two spare clips for the assault rifle.

Yezhov took them and slipped them into his jacket. The Russian boss checked the load on the rifle and gestured with a nod at the balcony. "I'm going up there. If someone comes through the door, let them. We catch them from above and behind."

The two men, their expressions neutral, nodded their understanding.

Minutes later, Yezhov was on the balcony. More discarded furniture littered the platform. He moved one of the tables to the edge of the balcony, setting it on its side, and crouched down behind the overturned furniture.

The tabletop likely wouldn't provide much protection if bullets flew in his direction, he realized. He just needed something to hide behind when his quarry arrived.

He glanced down at the lower level. A silhouette glided through the doorway. As the figure emerged from the shadows, Yezhov confirmed it was the American. He raised the rifle to his shoulder, lined his shot and curled the finger around the trigger.

BOLAN SLIPPED THROUGH the door and edged along the wall of the brief corridor leading into the pool area.

The soldier carried the M-4 at waist level, set in full-auto. Even as he stepped into the once-beautiful chamber, his combat senses began buzzing. Having learned long ago to listen to this built-in warning signal, the soldier slowed his gait and strained his other sense.

The place smelled bad—mildew. Otherwise, he detected nothing out of the ordinary—no traces of cologne, no stench of body odor or clothes that reeked of cigarette smoke. He heard water dripping somewhere in the chamber, slapping hard as though it fell several feet before striking a puddle.

As the soldier moved into the main chamber, the small hairs on the back of his neck stood up. Acting on instinct, he wheeled right and caught sight of one of the Yezhov's thugs swinging a shotgun muzzle toward him. Bolan caressed the trigger and his weapon spat out a fusillade of 5.56 mm fury that ripped into the man's chest. The man's finger tightened on the shotgun's trigger and it boomed once, the blast ripping into the air.

The soldier caught the partial reflection of a second shooter moving in a jagged length of mirror fixed to a nearby wall. The hardman was bringing an assault rifle's muzzle to bear on Bolan.

The soldier threw himself forward onto the ground. He rolled onto his back, locked his weapon's sights on the other man and cut loose with a fast burst from the M-4. The concentrated fire chewed the man's chest open, caused red geysers of blood to burst forth, before his body sank to the ground.

Ejecting the M-4's magazine, the soldier tossed it aside and grabbed another from his web gear. Before he could feed the magazine into the rifle, autofire erupted from above. Bullets hammered into the ceramic tiles covering the floor, pulverizing them and cutting a line toward the Executioner.

He hurled himself into another roll. In the same instant, he slammed home the magazine and chambered a round while moving across the floor. By this point the shooter had responded to Bolan's evasive moves. The line of autofire followed Bolan, ripping apart the floor like a buzz saw chewing through soft pine wood.

Bolan caught a break and was able to grab some cover behind one of the long-empty concrete planters situated around the room. The hard rain coming at Bolan pounded into the planter's exterior, eroding his cover. When a pause in the gunfire came, the soldier crawled around the side of the planter and, looking up at an angle, glimpsed Yezhov as the Russian withdrew from sight to reload his weapon.

Running in a zigzag pattern, Bolan squeezed off fast bursts that lanced out to the balcony. Slugs ripped into the tops of the overturned tables or struck the guard rails, sparking and whining off the steel. Yezhov popped into view unloading another blitz from his AK-47 and forcing Bolan to ground, taking refuge behind a waist-high wall that once had separated the kids' pool from the main one. Bullets pummeled the wall. Bolan's teeth ground together as he rode out the onslaught.

When the gunfire again subsided, the warrior popped up over the wall and fired off a round from the grenade launcher. The round arced and struck the floor of the balcony before it began spitting out white smoke.

The stairwell leading to the balcony lay a dozen or so yards ahead. With his adversary blinded, Bolan launched to his feet and closed the distance between himself and the stairs. The M-4 held level before him, he slipped through the door and up the stairs.

YEZHOV INSTINCTIVELY flinched when the metallic object struck the balcony. When plumes of white smoke began to hiss from it, he bit off a curse and loaded his final magazine into the AK-47. He guessed the American would be on the balcony in a matter of moments. Squinting, he scanned the smoke, eyes and rifle barrel moving in unison, but saw nothing. He knew better than to think his adversary had disappeared. Cooper might look for a strategic retreat if injured or absolutely overwhelmed by sheer numbers, but he wouldn't run from one man with an AK-47.

The big American had come for the woman, as Yezhov had guessed he would. But Yezhov had known that wouldn't be enough for the American. He would have been surprised and, yes, disappointed had the man pulled off a rescue and simply disappeared.

Between the Sindikat trying to hijack an American satellite program and snatching the woman, Yezhov guessed this man wanted his blood and wouldn't leave without spilling it.

Thus far, he had not disappointed Yezhov. Though the Russian had to admit he'd been surprised more than once by the American's seemingly boundless tenacity, skill and deadliness, not once had he been disappointed by the other man. And, considering that Cooper had nearly destroyed his empire, Yezhov would neither underestimate his adversary nor be sorry to see him go. No, like the bears that broke the rules of the hunt and killed their pursuers with sheer ferocity, Yezhov would destroy this man, leaving his bloodied corpse for the carrion to feast on.

The smoke stung his eyes, but had finally begun to dissipate, when Yezhov found the rear wall of the balcony. He edged along it, using it as a guide. Only one stairwell and one door led to and from the balcony. Cooper would have to use them. That meant Yezhov had to put himself within striking distance of that area without getting too close.

Motion in the corner of his eye caused Yezhov to whip his head right. A shadow, still hard to make out in the haze, was moving. With the AK snug against him, he twisted slowly, deliberately toward the shadowy form.

BOLAN CREPT THROUGH the door and onto the large balcony. The smoke had begun to dissipate so that he could at least distinguish the outlines of the overturned furniture closest to him. Something scratched against the smooth floor. Bolan tensed and stared into the smoke. A pair of rats scurried from hiding, splitting apart from one another and running around either side of the warrior.

Bolan exhaled. What had scared them from hiding? Him or Yezhov?

Reaching into his pocket, the Executioner drew out three spare 9 mm bullets. He tossed the shells to his right and they rattled across the floor.

A line of gunfire erupted from within the smoke, slicing the air just behind Bolan. The bullets flew close enough that the big American guessed Yezhov had seen him and wasn't just responding to Bolan's attempt at a distraction. The soldier dropped into a crouch and squeezed off a short salvo of 5.56 mm rounds toward the muzzle-flash. Yezhov responded by unleashing another torrent of autofire at Bolan. The soldier darted left and let loose with more autofire. He saw the other man's silhouette suddenly stiffen up and jerk in place under the onslaught from the M-4.

The Russian collapsed to the ground, his AK-47 clattering across the floor.

The M-4 at his shoulder, Bolan slowly closed in on the other man. Bolan saw Yezhov's fingers fumbling with a pistol holstered on his hip. The warrior tapped out a fast burst from the M-4. The rounds punched into the other man's skull and killed him.

20

Leo Turrin sat on his back patio on a cushioned chair, a large umbrella protecting him from the afternoon sun. The undercover Fed wore a flowered shirt, the tails hanging loose, hiding the .38 revolver fixed to his belt. The fabric of his white linen slacks rippled in the breeze blowing across his property. A plate with a half-eaten turkey sandwich and the crumbled remains of some potato chips stood on the table. Next to it was a glass filled with a splash of Scotch and two ice cubes. The bottle of Scotch, a bucket of ice and another glass lay within easy reach.

Turrin didn't usually drink at lunch. He preferred to keep his mind sharp for a couple of reasons. First, his ideal retirement didn't consist of an endless string of afternoons spent in a drunken stupor. Second, after decades of living a double life, it was a matter of preservation. It was a rare day when he didn't receive a phone call from one of his former mob colleagues, most of them retired, too, just looking to wile away some time talking about the old days. He'd woven a web of elaborate deceits both to gather information and to deflect suspicion. He hadn't made it this far only to blow everything with an ill-considered comment that sparked suspicion among his old colleagues.

He worried little about the repercussions for himself. Living on the edge as he had, Turrin had resigned himself to an early death. The resignation had allowed him to count every day he spent vertical as an undeserved blessing. So, no, the consequences for him carried little weight. But he had no illusions. Most of the people he'd consorted with over the years on the mob side of the ledger were human jackals. If they became suspicious of Turrin, they'd go after not only him, but also his family. Sure, if something happened to him, the Sarge would go scorched earth, exact payback that far exceeded the crime. But it wouldn't bring Turrin's family back.

So, yeah, he could forgo the afternoon cocktail most days. Today, though, he was treating himself to a drink. He'd just heard from Washington that he was in line for a meritorious service award from the attorney general for his undercover work. So he'd let himself have just one.

He picked up the glass, raised it to his lips. Before he could sip from it his phone trilled. He looked at the number flashing on the handset, swore under his breath and set down the drink. Duty called. The Executioner had asked him to tie up a loose end for him. Turrin had agreed to do so without hesitation.

He picked up the phone, but cast one last, longing look at the Scotch.

"Hello?"

"Leo Turrin. You son of a bitch," the voice on the other end said.

"Angelo Vacchi. I can't change my number fast enough to keep you away."

Vacchi, the retired head of La Cosa Nostra's East Coast operations, let go with a hearty laugh.

"Hey, I'm just returning the call. How you been, Leo?"

"Living the damn dream, my friend."

"That's the spirit, kid. Retirement treating you okay?"

"Be better if the old lady let me play more golf. I got in three days at the links last week. You believe that?"

"Unbelievable," Vacchi said.

"She wants me to take ballroom dancing lessons. You believe that?"

Vacchi laughed some more before it devolved into a smoker's hack. Turrin had heard through the grapevine that Vacchi had lung cancer, had retired because of it, in fact. Vacchi had installed his son into the throne, but word was the guy wasn't measuring up. Most of Turrin's golf matches over the last few weeks had been spent with other wise guys, trying to find out whether the younger Vacchi was about to get dethroned and, if so, who was going to take his place.

"Ballroom dancing? Good God, Leo the Pussy, ballroom dancing. Western civilization's crumbling before my eyes." He coughed twice more. When he spoke again, his voice sounded weaker. "So what'd you call me for, kid? You feeling nostalgic?"

"I come bearing gifts," Turrin said. "I got a nugget of information for you."

"Yeah?"

"Believe it. You know that crazy bitch, the one stealing all the money with the computers?"

"Sure, what'd they call her? Nighthawk?"

"Nightingale."

"Whatever. I heard she was on the run."

"Old news, buddy. She's on a slab," Turrin said.

"Dead? No shit."

"No shit."

"How you know this?"

"I'm clairvoyant," Turrin replied. His grin was audible in his voice. "You know me. I have sources."

"In other words, you're not going to tell me."

"Those are good words."

"Not many people, Leo, I let tell me no," Vacchi said.

"I don't ask for much, Angelo. And we both know who has your back," Turrin said, squelching an urge to cross his fingers. His eyes flicked to the digital recorder hooked into the phone.

"You're a good kid," Vacchi said. "Forget I asked. Hey, humor an old man and tell me what happened."

"That I can do." Turrin leaned back in his chair, set his feet on the table.

"And here's the reason I want to know," Vacchi interjected. "She stole money from me."

Turrin cocked his right eyebrow. "No kidding. How much she get?"

"Forget about it."

"C'mon, Angelo, just between us girls," Turrin said.

"Shit, Leo."

Turrin let a few seconds of silence build between them, knowing Vacchi wouldn't be able to keep his mouth shut.

"Three million dollars. She took three million dollars."

"Ouch."

"Tell me about it. Hell of it is, she stole it from one of my construction companies. Not a shell company. Nothing I was washing money with. Every penny of profit was legit."

"Damn," Turrin said, forcing himself to sound sympathetic.

"Once my accountants figured out the money was gone, I lost it. Not my finest moment. I figured it was an inside job, ordered my people to beat the bushes until they found the bastard who stole my money. Even hired a team of—what's the word?—forensic accountants to go over the books. We couldn't nail it one hundred percent, but there was one guy who made me suspicious. My guys sweated the little bastard, but he swore he didn't do it. I figured he was fucking with me. I had him, well, you know—"

"Dismissed."

"Exactly," Vacchi said.

"Don't worry. It's a secure phone."

"*You* I don't worry about, kid. A lot of these young fuckers coming up through the ranks, I sweat bullets over them. But not Leo Turrin."

"Thanks."

"So give. What happened?"

"Black Aces," Turrin said.

"Black Aces?"

"Black Aces. She was holed up in a little motel in a border town in south Texas. Place was abandoned—she was the only one inside. Black Ace got her location, swooped in and took her out."

"They get a body?"

"Pieces and parts. Apparently, the Ace shot her, cut off the extremities and took them with him. No teeth. No fingerprints. That'll make the Feds pound their heads against the wall, huh?"

"Serves them right. What'd he do with the hands?"

"Not sure. They're out their somewhere, probably hanging

from the guy's rearview mirror. Long and short, though, is the woman is dead and gone."

"We sure?"

"My source said he saw pictures of the head. It's all legit."

"And your source is?"

"Impeccable. Let's just say he lost even more than you did."

"The money?" Vacchi asked hopefully.

"Gone forever, I guess. Never a happy ending."

"Ah, hell, I'll take it, I guess. But a three-million-dollar bite leaves a hell of a scar."

"Understood."

Turrin heard a woman calling for Vacchi.

"Hey, gotta jump, Leo. The little lady's hollering for me."

The two men said their goodbyes and Turrin hung up the phone.

"You think he bought it?" a voice asked from behind. Even though Turrin recognized it almost immediately, the surprise still startled him. He twisted around in his chair until he could see the big man who'd sneaked up on him.

Mack Bolan, arms crossed over his chest, was leaning against the house. Mirrored aviator shades obscured his eyes. He was togged in a short-sleeved black polo shirt, dark blue jeans and black leather sneakers. Like Turrin, his shirttails hung loose well past his waist. Turrin assumed Bolan carried either the Beretta or the Desert Eagle holstered beneath the shirt.

"Thanks for that," Turrin said. "I'll go change my underwear now."

"Sorry," Bolan said. "I would have said something, but the thought of you dancing left me speechless."

"You heard that? You've been there that long?"

"I didn't want to distract a master in action."

"I can lay a line of B.S.," Turrin said. "Hope you learned a thing or two." He leaned forward and grabbed his drink. The ice cubes had nearly melted, eliciting a scowl from him. "Anyway, to answer your question, yeah, he bought it. For reasons I can't fathom, Angelo trusts me implicitly."

"You've done him a good turn along the way."

"Once or twice," Turrin said. He tossed the watered-down Scotch into the grass, set the empty glass on the wrought-iron table.

"He'll tell everyone else?" Bolan asked.

Turrin grinned. "Only everyone he sees or talks to on the phone. Angie has an unfiltered pipeline between his ears and his mouth. Everything that goes in the ears, comes out the mouth within a matter of minutes. I'll bet within twenty-four hours he's told a dozen people. And they'll tell a dozen more."

"And on and on."

"Right. If he actually understood the internet, he'd post it there."

Turrin leaned forward, poured himself two fingers of liquor into the glass, clawed a single cube from the ice bucket and dropped it into the drink. He poured his old friend an identical drink and slid it across the table to him.

"What about Wonderland?" Turrin asked, referring to Washington. "Are they leaving young Leo out here to do all the work?"

Bolan shook his head. "In a few hours, Brognola will issue a fake memo confirming her death. It will include most of the same details you just told Vacchi."

"In less colorful language."

"Naturally." Bolan picked up the Scotch, waved it under his nose. He rarely drank, but it smelled good. He took a small swallow, enjoyed the taste.

"You like?"

"I like."

"It's mob hooch. Hope that doesn't color your viewpoint on it."

"I'll try to look past it." He set the glass on the table, but not too far out of reach. "The memo will name another Black Ace as the source. That takes the focus off you."

Turrin whistled. "You're going to finger an Ace as a mole? He's dead meat."

Bolan shrugged. "He's a mad dog. Got a victim list as long as my arm. Good riddance. The CIA also plans to issue a top-secret briefing to other intelligence agencies. That goes to the State Department's intelligence analysis shop. They'll circulate a classified briefing to their various outposts, demanding that it be kept hush-hush."

"Thereby setting the stage for it to get leaked."

"Bingo," Bolan said.

"Okay, so since rumors of her death are greatly exaggerated, what next? You think she can start over?"

"I hope so," Bolan said. "After all she's been through, she deserves a little peace."

JENNIFER DAVIS POSED in front of the full-length mirror in her bedroom and studied her look. A black skirt cut just above the knees sheathed her hips and thighs. Skin tanned golden from the Arizona sun caused her white, sleeveless blouse to gleam. Her hair, dyed a deep red, was tied into a long ponytail.

She turned once and noticed the muscles ripple gently in her calves as she did. Her stomach and biceps were toned. Even by her own exacting standards, she looked great, better than she had in years. Spending six months in a secluded safe house with nothing to do but eat, exercise and read did that for a person.

There had been the hours-long debriefings by a team of intelligence analysts from the Treasury Dept., FBI, CIA and NSA. Nothing came for free. But she'd had plenty of time to heal her body and mind, if not her soul.

Now here she was in Baltimore, Maryland, getting dressed for her first day of work. Excitement and anxiety fluttered in her stomach, vied for her attention. She hadn't held an actual, honest-to-God day job in years. But a new group made up of spooks from multiple agencies, one aimed at tracking terrorist financing, was revving up. The government had made Davis a sweet offer, one she'd jumped on. New identity, new job. She'd still live in the shadows to some extent, but not as she had.

She thought briefly of Matt Cooper, felt a warm sensation of gratitude for the guy. He'd kept his word, every last syllable. He'd had her back, just like he'd promised. He'd come for her when Yezhov had snatched her, not because he thought she was a weak damsel, but because that's what he'd promised. And he'd made good on his oath that she'd return to at least some kind of normal life. She hadn't heard from the big guy since they'd flown back to a small commercial airport in Virginia months ago. He'd handed her over to a small cadre of men from the DOJ, including a man named Hal Brognola, who chewed through cigars like chewing gum. Judging by the deference paid to him by the others in the group—which included the Director of National Intelligence and the directors of the FBI and CIA—Brognola was the highest of high rollers in the government's security hierarchy, if not in title then in the authority and respect he commanded from those around him.

She'd pressed Brognola for more information about Cooper. After a half-dozen times, Brognola pulled his unlit, but well-chewed cigar into an ashtray and shot her a no-nonsense look across the table.

"Here's some advice," Brognola said. "You're living a new life now. You'll never, ever forget the people from the old one. It's possible you won't ever speak of them. But you'll never forget them, nor should you. They're one of the reasons you did all the things you did, why you're here today."

She opened her mouth to speak. He gestured her to stay quiet and she complied.

"But forget about Matt Cooper," Brognola said. "Don't talk about him to anyone, no matter their security clearance or rank. No veiled references. No stories with what you consider important details omitted. If anyone asks, you never heard of the guy. Consider him like Santa Claus, he doesn't exist. Not that it will ever happen, but if you ever get hauled in front of Congress over that business in England and Russia? It was Navy SEALS who pulled your fat out of the fire. Understood?"

"Why?"

"It's the only way he can do what he does. It's the only way he can help others like he helped you. Trust me, this is bigger than either of us."

After a brief pause, she nodded tentatively. "Okay."

"Don't screw with me on this."

She scowled. "All right, I won't. I promise."

Apparently satisfied, Brognola turned the conversation in another direction. She'd kept her promise that day and knew she always would. At least to a point. She'd never mention Matt Cooper, ever, especially if it would put him at risk. But she wouldn't forget him or what he'd done for her, either. He hadn't just saved her life, he'd given her a new one. He'd forever have her loyalty for that.

* * * * *